Rescued by the Cowboy Books

(Sweet Clean Christian Western Romance)

By J. A. Somers

Rescued by the Cowboy at Christmas Collection Books 1-4

Rescued by the Cowboy at Christmas, Volume 6

J. A. Somers

Published by J. A. Somers, 2023.

This is a work of fiction. Similarities to real people, places, or events are entirely coincidental.

RESCUED BY THE COWBOY AT CHRISTMAS COLLECTION BOOKS 1-4

First edition. August 9, 2023.

Copyright © 2023 J. A. Somers.

ISBN: 979-8223821960

Written by J. A. Somers.

Table of Contents

Cowboy under the Mistletoe: Rescued by the Cowboy at Christmas Book 1

(Sweet Clean Christian Western Romance)
By J. A. Somers

Books by J. A. Somers

Rescued by the Cowboy at Christmas
Cowboy Under the Mistletoe
Cowboy's Christmas Blessing
Cowboy for Christmas
Cowboy's Christmas Wish

Cowboy Under the Mistletoe

A cowboy with a broken heart. An ex-fiancée with a secret...

Carter Charming stopped celebrating the holidays after his fiancée, Paige, left him without a word. So he swore he'd never marry, never date, and he avoided mistletoes like it was going out of style. But when the magic of Christmas flows over the small town of Mistletoe and his mother plays a little matchmaking, will this stubborn cowboy change his mind?

Chapter 1

A wave of anxiety swept through Paige Louisa as the snow flurries fell harder on her windshield. Her pulse pounded hard inside her chest.

Charlie.

I have to find Charlie.

Where is he?

Why did he run off like that?

Oh, Lord please keep him safe out there.

He had to be somewhere around the area. Where could he be right now? Why did this have to happen?

Paige's visibility tapered off by the minute as she drove slowly down the road passing colorful bright lights and Christmas decorations on this dark winter night. She was feeling anything but festive right now.

The town of Mistletoe was known for its brutal winter storms. And she just had to be visiting now.

He couldn't have gotten far, could he? Her friend Daphne was in tears when she told Paige that Charlie had ran off. Paige had left Charlie at her friend's house while she went into town.

She prayed to God to help her find him before anything happened to him.

Paige was beginning to wonder if coming back to Mistletoe was a mistake.

She agreed to come back to town to help out with the Annual Christmas sleigh ride for the kids at the hospital.

After her father passed recently, she thought it would be a good idea. Especially since Christmas would be in four weeks.

She didn't want to be alone. This was also the time of the year her mother passed, two years ago. And now her father passed before Christmas. She believed her dad died of a broken heart. His wife and best friend of 40 years was gone. Seeing her die slowly had crushed his soul and his spirit. Paige had left Mistletoe to go back to her home city in Texas to spend time with him to help him to heal.

She'd left Mistletoe at that time. And she had to break up with her now former fiancé without so much as a word. Even though it tore her up inside to do that, she felt she had no other choice. She never did get to explain why.

If he found out about her, he probably wouldn't want anything to do with her. So it was for the best.

Still, memories of spending Christmas with her ex-fiancé Carter and his family flooded her mind with a warm feeling.

His family really knew how to celebrate the holidays. They always went all out with the best decorations; brightest lights and they even hosted the Annual sleigh ride with the huskies. Her stomach knotted with anxiety thinking she might see him again. But she couldn't think about that right now. She hadn't even planned to step foot back in Mistletoe until now.

Daphne also encouraged her to come back to Mistletoe for the lighting of the town Christmas Tree, the most beautiful tree in the county. The mayor had also invited her to come too. She'd designed the new Children's Play Center at the Mistletoe Children's Hospital. She was an interior designer and submitted her entry during a contest. She always loved making things beautiful. Too bad those skills didn't translate to her love life.

Her design had won a prestigious award and she'd become a bit of a local celebrity for her innovative approach to making a place calm, entertaining and relaxing at the same time. Her Instagram page had hundreds of thousands of likes. But what her followers didn't know was that she was anything but happy.

She'd moved from small town Mistletoe to her home city be closer to her mother when she became ill. And then she stayed to take care of her father. But while she was there she'd facetimed her then fiancé and told him she couldn't go through with the wedding. She thought she could let him down easy. But there was nothing easy about breaking up with the man who was supposed to be the love of your life. Carter Charming, a tall and handsome cowboy who lived up to his last name.

Carter was Mistletoe's beloved cowboy running the famous Charming Ranch, a ranch resort in the small town of Mistletoe. She knew she'd become an enemy of the town for breaking his heart. Small town close-knit community meant everybody knew everybody's business. And she couldn't even tell him the real reason why she left him—she couldn't tell *anyone*.

He'd leave you anyway if he really found out about you.

She found out something about herself when she went back home. It was something she couldn't share with Carter.

Just then as Paige's car hit a bump in the road. She swerved over to the side; her tires slid into the ditch.

Oh, no.

She was stuck.

There was practically zero visibility with the snowfall. She was practically in the middle of nowhere.

Would anyone find her in time?

If she stepped out of her car, she might freeze to death, but if she stayed inside, she wouldn't be any better off, would she?

She'd heard about what happened to that couple who stayed in their car and froze. But then again, was it because they didn't turn on the heat for five minutes every hour?

Numbness filled Paige's body.

How would she find Charlie now?

What if she died? What if this was it?

What was she going to do now?

She prayed to the Lord to protect her, to show her a way out. But she had a sinking feeling it might be too late?

***

Carter Charming paused and watched as the pretty snowflakes fell hard over Charming Ranch, his family's ranch in Mistletoe. He then went back to his task, fixing the Christmas lights on the barn.

Sadness swept over him when he thought about how much he missed his dear dad. His father and he used to put up the lights on the barn at this time of the year. His father made living on the ranch a lot of fun for his sons.

It had been one year now since his old man's passing. And he missed him like crazy. Christmas at Charming Ranch Resort was a magical time of the year for the town. They went all out and decorated the land to make it festive. It was special because they often invited members of the community to join in the celebrations. Especially kids from the treatment center nearby.

It should be a beautiful sight, but instead it brought sad memories. Reminders of what was, and what could have been.

He could hear the sound of laughter and singing coming from the newly renovated barn hall. He should have been decorating the ranch with the love of his life—but she was gone.

He should feel the magic, but he only felt sorrow right now. He wished he could feel the magic, but that was all lost when his fiancée walked out on him. Her name was Paige. She was everything to him. He really thought he had a future with her.

He prayed to the Lord to give him strength to get over what happened, but he wondered if he'd never feel love again. His prayers seemed to go unanswered. He'd asked God to help him to forgive her what she did to him that night. Trust was always a big thing for him. Without it there was nothing. And she'd broken his trust. She left him without telling him why.

Even though she'd broken his heart and betrayed his trust. He still loved her. Missed her. Wished he could make things right with her. But that was never going to happen now. He just couldn't see himself falling in love again and trusting another woman.

Right now, the Charmings, his wonderful family, were preparing for the church Christmas play. Then in a few days, the lighting of the town Christmas tree. This time of the year seemed to keep his mind too busy to worry about anything else.

"You're not done yet?" his brother Noel teased him. "Just kidding. Looks great, cowboy."

"Thanks, bro."

"What's on your mind?" Noel asked him perceptively.

"What makes you think anything's on my mind?" Carter asked.

"Come on, cowboy? I know what you're thinking."

"And what's that?"

"That you're going to try to skip out on the annual Christmas dance."

His brother was right.

Just then his mother, Lucinda walked in cheerfully, dressed in Christmas colors, wearing one of those ugly sweaters with the reindeer lights flashing.

Carter couldn't help but grin. His mother was the town's biggest Christmas cheerleader. She'd grown the boys to love giving and sharing and to cherish the true meaning of the holiday. Sometimes the best Christmas gifts were not wrapped under the tree, but what's wrapped around the heart, the love you give to others.

"You are coming to the dance this time, aren't you, Carter?" His mother arched a brow, with a grin on her lips.

"You know, I'm not one for all that celebration, Ma."

"Oh, come on now. How else are you going to meet someone?"

"Maybe, I don't want to. I already did and it didn't work out."

"Oh, darling. You know I'm so sorry about what happened between you and Paige, but you have to move on. You know the Lord will give you beauty for your ashes."

That's what the good book said, but right now, Carter had a hard time getting over what happened to what he thought was the best relationship he ever had.

Was it something he said? Did? He just didn't get it. The rejection and abandonment left a gaping hole in his heart. He and Paige had a large engagement party. Everything seemed fine. He'd never been so close to anyone before.

What was she hiding from him?

Carter shifted his thoughts back to the present.

His mother was right. Christmas was about love, giving, remembering the birth of Jesus. But right now, he couldn't put his head around the fact that he was broken-hearted and humiliated. His pride took a beating when she dumped him before their nuptials.

And she broke up with him around the Christmas season too. A sign that maybe the holidays wasn't meant for everyone. Especially not for him.

He and Paige dreamed of having a family of their own. Three kids and a dog. A border collie rescue. They'd had it all planned out. But it didn't work out that way and he felt that he must have done something wrong to deserve that.

It took a lot out of him to be close to anyone. After all, his own family abandoned him before the Charmings adopted him as a child.

Carter was crushed to pieces.

"It's snowing pretty hard out there," Noel said. "We'd better finish up later."

The visibility decreased with each heavy snowfall. As they got ready to go back to the main house, Carter paused.

Just then his attention turned to the roadside. He saw a car in the distance.

"What are you looking at?" Noel asked.

"Do you see that?"

"See what?" Noel looked but couldn't see much.

"I could swear I saw blinkers."

"Blinkers?"

"Looks like someone's in a ditch somewhere. I'm going to go out there."

"You want me to come with you? Snow's coming down hard."

"Nah, I'll be all right."

Carter then got into his pickup truck and made his way out to the road.

Before long he came to a snowbank where he saw a blue sedan stuck. There was a woman beside the car, shivering, trying to make a phone call.

She then turned around and called out, "Charlie! Charlie!"

Her hood covered her face. Snow flurries swirled around them.

"You all right, ma'am?" Carter asked. "You need help?"

The woman wore a parker winter jacket with an oversized faux fur trimmed hood. Her face was barely visible. Long strands of ebony hair peeked through the sides of her hood as it swayed with the heavy gusts of wind.

"I'm fine," she said, then frantically shouted, "Charlie!"

"You're looking for your friend?"

"Sorry, I'm just...I was looking for my dog. He's a husky rescue. He.... he ran off from my friend's house."

"Ma'am, I'm sorry about that. I'll help you look for him. Where was he last seen?"

"I was driving around but my car's dead. So's my phone."

"I'll get someone to look at your car for you, but you really shouldn't be out here by yourself right now. Storm's going to get worse. You're in luck, you can use my phone and I'll drive you around to find Charlie."

"Thanks. I really appreciate it. Though I don't feel so lucky right now."

Carter paused for a moment. The woman's voice sounded familiar.

He liked the sound of her voice. He didn't know why. But something inside him resonated with it. She had a soft yet warm voice and strong.

Wait a minute...

It couldn't be her...

As if she read his mind, the woman lifted her hood slightly so that she could get a look at him.

The snowflakes began to let down a little, but she looked like a pretty Christmas portrait. Her lips were red like strawberries, her lovely dark hair silky and wavy, her eyes were lovely, framed by long thick lashes. She looked precious. Like a breathtaking cover model. He could tell by her hip hugging parka jacket that she still had those lovely curves. Her legs seemed to go on for ever. She wore a slim fitted pants with long leather snow boots.

But she looked mortified when their eyes met.

"Oh, my goodness! Carter!" she said, her eyes wide with surprise.

"Paige," was all he said. He didn't know what to feel right now.

Paige was there.

He never thought he'd ever lay eyes on her pretty face again. But as the snow melted on his face, so did the anger he'd felt when she walked out on him.

She smiled. "Thank you, Carter. And thanks for rescuing me out here."

"Hey, it's no trouble. I just happened to spot your flashing lights in the distance."

"You've got good vision."

Good vision?

He wished he had good vision when it came seeing into the future.

Talk about love being blind.

And speaking of blind. He knew he couldn't afford to be blindsided by his beautiful ex-fiancée again.

Carter, focus.

Okay, so he had no idea where his thoughts were going right now, but he had to do the right thing.

Carter escorted Paige to his Ford pickup truck and closed the passenger side door when she got in.

He then made his way over to the driver's side, the heavy gusts of wind moving faster and faster again, snow falling fast once more.

"We'll find Charlie." His voice was confident. He hoped he found her husky in time.

"Thanks, Carter. I really appreciate this." She bit down on her lower lip. He loved when she did that. But he had to shift his focus.

"So when did you adopt Charlie?"

Did she choose companionship with a dog instead of him?

"After Mom passed, Dad was in a state. Well, we rescued Charlie from the shelter and...well, he's been the best thing for Dad and me. He's very protective and full of energy.

"How is your dad?"

"He...he passed away."

"Man, I'm really sorry to hear that."

"Thank you. He never got over Mom passing and seeing her suffer before she died broke his heart."

"I can just imagine."

As he started the car, the engine wouldn't budge.

"What's wrong?" Paige asked.

"Everything," he said, matter-of-factly. "Looks like we're both stuck now."

Chapter 2

"I'm worried about Carter," Lucinda said to her sister Nellie as they fixed ornaments on the Christmas tree at the main house.

Nellie glanced out the window looking at the flurries of snow falling heavy outside. "Oh, don't worry. Carter's good on the road. He'll be safe."

"Oh, no not that. I know he'll be fine there. I'm just worried he's given up."

"Given up?"

"Yes. He's going to skip the annual Christmas dance again."

"Oh no."

"His father's death really hit him hard. You know Cam and Carter were inseparable. Then his fiancée broke up with him."

"Yes, that was awful."

"I know. He never got over the fact that she didn't give him a reason why she left him."

"Yes, that was terrible, wasn't it?"

"I tried to tell Carter not to give up. That the Lord will give him beauty for his ashes and that everything happens for a reason. He hasn't even been to church in a while. Carter has so much love to give. He's such a good man. I really hope he would start going out again and seeing people."

"He will. I will talk to him."

"I don't think that will help. He won't listen to anyone."

"What you need to do is get him out on a blind date. Have you ever thought of that?"

"No. And I know he won't go for it."

"Look at us two, plotting to get Carter matched up."

"Well, all my boys are single right now. I know they've had their share of heartbreak but I don't want them to give up on love."

"You know something," her sister said. "I think they just might need a little help along."

Lucinda gave her sister a sly look as she watched her thinking. She could practically see the wheels in her sister's head turning.

"You know something?" Nellie said, twirling an ornament of an angel in her hand. "I think I know what to do."

"And what's that?" Lucinda asked, taking the ornament from her sister's hand and placing it strategically on the tree.

It was a large Christmas tree, a very special tree with a special story behind it. They had just started to decorate it and it would probably take a while.

"You know sister Sue Ellen from the church?"

"Yes?" Lucinda said cautiously.

"Well, her daughter is single. She's just been through a divorce and I heard she's looking for husband number two.

"Oh, is that so?"

"Yes, that's so."

"But what do you know about Sue Ellen's daughter? I mean, is she nice? And is she honest? You know Carter has this thing about honesty. He can't deal with anyone else pulling the wool over his eyes. I mean who could blame him after what happened to him."

"I know, darling sis. Just leave the rest to me. Trust me. I'm the matchmaker of the church."

"You are?"

"Yes. I got Graham and Lilly together. Remember?"

"You did that?"

"Well, kind of. I mean they came to my rescue when I fell after that heatwave, remember. I was singing in the choir and I just collapsed from the heat."

"Oh, right. I remember, the air conditioner had broken down at the church during that heatwave."

"Exactly."

"But how did you get those two together?" Lucinda arched her brow.

"They both came to my rescue and got me into an air-conditioned car. And they stayed with me. I was out of it at the time but then they ended up talking to each other."

"Nellie!"

"What?"

Her old sister was a hoot. Sometimes. She was seventy. Ten years older than Lucinda. But she loved her big sis.

"So what do you plan to do? Faint in front of Carter and Sue Ellen's daughter?"

They both laughed. Then...

They heard a loud bang and the electricity went out.

"Oh, no."

"A blackout. Great. That's all we need."

"Now I'm really worried about Carter," Lucinda said.

"Don't worry, he'll find someone. I'll see to it."

"No. He's out there helping a stranded driver. And now it looks as if the town's blacked out." She glanced out the window frantic, seeing nothing but darkness.

"I hope he'll be okay. Anything can happen."

There was no power. Now Lucinda was about to have panic attack.

Chapter 3

Carter didn't want to worry Paige. He wanted to help her find her dog, Charlie. A surge of duty rushed through him to protect her, to help her, to keep her safe. The truth was, he never stopped caring for darling Paige. Even though she crushed his heart when she broke off their engagement over a Christmas holiday—of all time.

He moved the steering wheel to turn the tires to make them straight then he got out of the car. He could see snow accumulating faster than a speeding bull.

He cleared a path around his tires and tried to dig snow away from them. He couldn't believe how fast the snow accumulated in that short time.

Mistletoe was famous for its winter storms. That's why he always made sure he was prepared. He moved around to the back to get a shovel.

"Can I help?" Paige offered, getting out of the truck, her hair swaying in the heavy gusts of wind. She looked like a snow angel.

"Please, let me help," she offered again.

That's darling Paige for you, always willing to help.

"I'm good. Thanks for the offer though."

He was dying to ask her what she was thinking walking out on him?

Why did she leave him?

Why didn't she return any of his calls?

Did she meet someone new? Was that it?

Did the Lord bring her back to him for a reason, so he could have closure before he moved on?

She'd left to take care of her father, after her mother passed, but she never came back. She told him she would be moving back to her home city. But now she's back in Mistletoe. He had so many questions to ask her, but right now, they had other priorities like finding Charlie and getting out of the snowstorm.

Was this some sort of sign? Was the Lord trying to get Carter and Paige back together?

He didn't think so. Maybe it was just a coincidence. After all, the man upstairs knew how much he was broken by her leaving him. Maybe she was going to apologize or explain why. But he didn't want to get his hopes up.

Right now, he had to make sure he got her to safety and find her pooch.

Then maybe he'll stay away from her.

After all, this could only spell trouble, right?

She had plenty of time to call him over the past two years to let him know what the deal was, but she didn't.

He knew she was going through a lot after her mom passed, but he wanted to be there for her, to help her through it, but she wouldn't let him.

She hugged herself as she walked over to him. He could tell she was shivering slightly. He wanted to reach out and give that bear hug, like he used to give her, to let her know everything would be all right.

"Are you sure? I mean we're in this together. You saved me just now, and you're helping me look for Charlie. I want to do something."

"Okay, if you want, you can get behind the steering wheel and touch the gas when I tell you to."

"Sounds good," she said and got into the driver's side of his truck.

Just then the power in the city went out. They were pitched into darkness on the road, save for his headlights.

"Oh, no," she said after she wound down the window. "Power outage. What's going to happen now? There's no visibility."

She was right.

They were in more trouble now than before.

How were they going to get to Charlie? What were they going to do now?

Between the heavy gusts of snow and the darkness, they were in more danger if they ended up skidding into goodness knew what.

He knew during a winter storm the best advice was to stay home. Well, they were quite a ways from home right now.

He knew they had to stay warm and stay safe. He checked out his cell phone and the battery level was at five per cent.

He'd been busy all day and hadn't had a chance to charge it yet.

This was nothing. He served his time in the military. Getting out of sticky situations was his thing.

Survival was the key. Being prepared for anything was important. Carter lived by that. He was prepared for anything, well physically, not where his heart was concerned.

"Right now, we've got to keep safe," he said.

She got out of the truck and moved closer to him. He then reached over to hug her and she hugged him back.

He felt a tingling sensation down his spine, was that the cold? Or was that his feelings for Paige?

She smiled up at him. "Thank you. You feel so warm."

"No problem."

He had extra food and water in his truck, a flashlight, shovel, battery supply and some first aid supplies, and a blanket. Thank goodness for that.

Carter said a silent prayer to the man upstairs that he'd take them safely back to the ranch in this messy storm. He wished he could pray the storm away, but he knew that it was better that they stay safe. He knew storms happened all the time, especially storms in your life.

His old man once told him that the Lord could get them through any adversity, if they believed and never gave up hope.

"What should we do?" she asked, snuggling closer into him.

"You want a blanket? I've got one in the truck."

"That would be great, thanks."

He walked her back to the truck as the wind blew against them and swirling snow decreased their visibility. He held onto her to keep her steady. Once she was in the truck. He made his way into the driver's seat and closed the door shut, the wind howling around them. He then reached back for the blanket in the backseat and wrapped it around her.

"Thank you. You really are a hero in a time of need."

"Just prepared. My old man used to tell us to be prepared for anything."

"He was special, wasn't he?" she said.

"He sure was. I really miss him. Thought he'd be around forever."

Sorrow swept over Carter. Not only for the loss of his dad, but for the loss of his fiancée. For the future he thought they'd have.

If this was a sign that he could have a second chance with her at all, then it was a strange sign.

Paige looked down. He couldn't tell but she seemed as sorry as he was.

"Anyway, the best thing right now would be to stay in the truck and keep warm," he said. "I'll turn on the heat once in a while—just for 10 minutes to keep us warm, then open the window so we don't get carbon monoxide issues then shut off the engine. We'll wait until the storm dies down a bit then we can search for Charlie."

"Sounds good. I just hope he'll be all right out there." She hesitated as if she wanted to say something more. Then she stopped and looked away.

"Siberian Huskies are resilient," he added. "They can withstand the most frigid temperatures. He'll be all right. We just have to get to him."

"Thank you. You're right." She huddled up in the front seat after they switched and he sat back in the driver's chair.

She then started singing *Silent Night*. Her voice was soft and beautiful and melodic.

"You know that's my favorite song," he said, an appreciative smile curving his lips.

She turned to him and said, "I know. It's *our* favorite song. It *was* our favorite song."

"Yes, it was."

She looked into his eyes.

A sweet shiver danced down his spine.

He had to ignore those feelings. He shouldn't get his hopes up.

This was one cowboy that wasn't going to be suckered into that romance thing again. He'd vowed he'd never marry, never get involved seriously with another woman after Paige left him.

He thought they'd connected so well in the past. They looked out for each other. She was his rock and he was hers. Or so he thought.

He always wondered if she left him for another man. Was that it? Did she find someone else in her home city when she went back home to take care of her mother and then her father?

Torn.

That's how he felt right now. He sure wished the Lord would give him another sign. A clear sign on what to do now. He wanted to be angry with her. But he just couldn't. His heart melted every time she was near him.

Butterflies exploded in his belly when she brushed her hand against his, like when he handed her the blanket just a while ago. And that sweet intoxicating scent of her perfume wafted to his nostrils. He always loved her scent. He always loved everything about her. Except what she did to him two years ago. Around a Christmas holiday.

It was just a few weeks before Christmas when she broke off with him then.

She was the reason he'd stopped celebrating the holidays.

And now?

She was back. Around the holidays.

Christmas.

It was the time of year to celebrate the birth of Christ. It was also a time for family, love, good home cooking, feasts, festive celebrations, Christmas lights, snowball fights, sleigh rides in the snow, Christmas plays, dances, love in the air. And unity.

He and Paige always celebrated the holidays together. They always went all out for a fun time.

They'd sang at a Christmas concert once. His mom said they sounded like two angels in love.

Well, that was then, not now.

"What's on your mind?" she finally asked him. Her pretty eyes wide and innocent looking.

"Nothing."

"Nothing? Oh, come on now. You look like you have the world on your shoulders, Carter. I know you."

"Do you?" he asked, softly.

"Hey..."

"Sorry, I just...It's been a while, hasn't it?"

"Yes, it has."

There was that awkward silence between them. What was he going to do now?

"You left without saying a word," he finally said.

There he said it.

She turned to face him again, a look of shock on her face.

Chapter 4

"What?" Paige asked, stunned.

They both sat in his pickup as the snow fell hard outside, blanketing the town in a coat of white. The stars blinked in the dark night sky. But they weren't the only things that blinked.

Paige didn't think she heard right.

"You think I left you without saying a word? Is that what you *believe*?"

"Whoa! Wait a minute, now." Carter adjusted his cowboy hat. "I'm really sorry about what happened to your mom. That's terrible." His voice broke. "I wanted to help, but you told me to stay put."

She glanced down at her hands; heat climbed to her cheeks.

She couldn't tell him the real reason. She just couldn't. He wouldn't understand. He'd want to stay far away from her.

Truth was, she'd been miserable away from him. She missed Mistletoe. She missed the ease of the country life. The simple life. The wide-open spaces. The sweet cozy small town where everybody knew your name and they all cared about you. They welcomed you in with open arms every time. Unlike the big city. The city seemed so distant. So far away. Especially since she lost her mother and now her father.

Something terrible happened when Paige went back to Little Heart, Texas to take care of her mother and then her father.

That was the reason she had to break up with Carter.

She silently asked the Lord to forgive her for not coming clean with him right now. She also prayed for the wisdom to do what's right.

Oh, why was she so confused?

"Then," he continued. "After she passed, after the funeral, you said you needed to stay with your dad for a while to help him through it. That was two years ago. I waited for you, like you asked me to. Then I get this letter saying we should cool it off. What was that about? You even changed your phone number..."

Her stomach knotted into nerves. He was right. She hadn't been fair to him, but she had no choice.

"Carter, I..."

"Paige, what happened between us?" he asked, his voice so sweet and soft. "We were so happy together. You said we were meant to be together. We were so good together. We had so much fun whenever we were in the same room. You were my soul mate. I thought I was yours."

"You are...I mean you were..." She looked off, stung by humiliation.

He was right, and she knew it.

Should she tell him the real reason why?

Would he be upset? Would he understand?

"I *was*...?" he echoed.

"You still are, Carter. I mean...well, you know what I mean."

"No, I don't, Paige. Tell me." His voice was gentle and warm.

She paused for a moment. Her heartbeat galloped in her chest like a bucking bull at a rodeo.

"I can't tell you, Carter. I've never stopped love.... I mean, you'll always mean something to me, but we just can't be together." She turned to stare out at the falling snowflakes, so pretty against the night sky as the wind blew dancing flurries around the pick-up truck. She hoped he wouldn't press any further.

Her heart pounded hard inside her, wishing she didn't have to face him again. The last things she wanted to do was to hurt him. Again.

Carter and she could never be together and that's all he had to know. He didn't need to know the reason. Not the *real* reason.

If he ever found out about her, he wouldn't want anything to do with her.

Chapter 5

Carter could not believe this.

This was not how he'd planned this Saturday night. He was supposed to be helping his family with the decorations for the Christmas barn dance that would take place in a few weeks. And that would be his only part in the family holiday tradition—the decorating. He wasn't planning on being a part of the festivities.

A thought crept into his mind, his mother's words. She really wanted him to be the mistletoe cowboy this year. But that just wasn't going to happen. In fact, he was going to be the only cowboy to *not* kiss under the mistletoe.

He had no idea he'd meet up with the reason he stopped celebrating the holidays. And now? She was distancing from him again. What was she hiding?

What could be so bad?

"Is someone hurting you?" he asked, concerned. If anyone caused this pretty lady any kind of distress, he would have a few words with this guy.

"No. It's...it's not that."

"Are you sure? Look me in the eyes."

She turned to face him.

Those pretty eyes of hers gazed into his. For a moment, his heart turned over in his chest. She always had that effect on this cowboy. Every time. Even though they'd been apart for the past couple years, he never stopped thinking about her, dreaming about her, obsessing about her, wondering if she was okay.

"Carter, it's complicated," she finally spoke through those beautiful shapely lips of hers. And he was dying to press his lips to hers again.

The memory of their kisses lingered in his heart all these years. She was special. No other woman in his life had ever had that kind of effect on him. So what went wrong? What was she hiding from him? What could be so bad that she didn't want to tell him?

"I thought you and I could talk about anything," he said.

"We could." She looked away, her eyes misty.

"You okay?"

"Yes."

"You don't look okay."

He wanted to tell her how he felt. That he never stopped loving her too. That's what she was going to say earlier before she stopped, wasn't it?

But he'd been burned before. No way was he going to share his feelings with his ex, only for her to turn around and throw it back in his face, like she did when she left him.

Just then, the lights in the town went back on.

"Oh, hallelujah!" she said. "Praise the Lord. Now we can see."

He grinned. Her expressions, the way she said "hallelujah" always got to him in a sweet way. Her voice was angelic.

He wasn't going to stop until he found out what was hurting her. Or *who's* hurting her.

"Yeah, it looks as if we're out of the dark."

Carter started up the engine again and drove his truck down the roadside. They were out of the dark in the storm, but they were still in the dark when it came to what was keeping them apart.

Now, he just had to ask the man upstairs to give him another sign. Should he leave things be? Or not? Somehow he believed that maybe she was back so that he could finally have closure and move on. But then again, why was his heart behaving differently from his mind?

Chapter 6

"Good! Now, we can look for Charlie!" Paige and Carter spoke at the same time.

She gushed.

They always said things at the same time as if they shared one mind, one heart.

A grin curved that handsome cowboy's lips. She always loved the way his lips looked.

He chuckled. "Looks like we're always thinking the same thing."

"So true. That used to annoy everyone when we spoke like that."

Paige kept her eyes peeled to the roadside, looking around for her thick furry husky. She loved Charlie more than anything. It would crush her spirit if anything ever happened to him. But Carter was right, Charlie was resilient. It was in his nature. The only trouble was that this husky had been through emotional distress when she'd rescued him from the shelter. He'd been abandoned by his previous family.

The thought pierced her heart.

Focus, Paige. She had to focus on getting to Charlie.

She felt a connection to her dog. He'd given her dad so much love and companionship, but he was also Paige's best friend. A friend that would never leave her. No matter what.

She turned around to look at the other side of the road as the truck moved slowly on the snow-covered ground and saw Carter's eyes fixed on the road scanning around for her dog.

What would she do without Carter right now?

Guilt swept through her as she thought of how she had to end it with him. She wanted to spare him any heartbreak, that's why she broke up with him. But she inadvertently ended up bestowing heartbreak on this handsome cowboy anyway. That was not her intention.

"It might be hard to find him," Paige said, swallowing hard. Her faith waned with each distance they drove.

Charlie was nowhere to be seen.

"We'll find him," Carter said, his voice sounding determined, hopeful.

She'd always loved that about him. He was a man in charge that took control when things got rough in the past. And this cowboy had a tough can-do attitude.

Her heart galloped in her chest at the thought.

Man, she missed him. She missed being around him, hugging him, kissing him, spending time with him. So why was she keeping that secret away from him?

Because she had no choice. It was for the best.

Funny, how things that felt like the best decision, didn't make her feel too good.

"Hey, wait a minute," Carter said, narrowing his eyes to focus on something in the distance. "What's that over there?"

"What? I don't see anything." Except a gallon of flurries falling hard to the ground. The sky looked like a pretty collage of snowflakes. Mistletoe was known for its snowy weather and brisk winds.

"Over there." Carter pointed. His eyes fixed on something.

Carter always had good eyesight. This cowboy had the sharpest vision she'd ever seen.

He could spot a dot from a mile away, she thought.

Carter pulled over to the side.

"Stay here, I'm going to see what's out there."

"Oh, no. I want to come with you."

"Are you sure?"

"We'd be together. That's all that counts."

She couldn't read his expression. Was that of surprise or sadness?

Oh great. She told him they'd be together but he knew it only meant right now.

She'd also told him that "we'd always be together and that's what count" in the past when they became engaged.

And now she said it again, but it had a different meaning.

"Okay, just stay close to me," he said as he got out of the truck, closing the door behind him. He then went to her side and opened the door. She'd always loved his chivalry.

"I see something over there by the lake." He grabbed some rope and tools out of the back of his pick-up.

Heart pounding with adrenaline, Paige watched then offered to help.

"It's all right. I just need you to hold on to the end of the rope.

"You think it's Charlie?"

"I'm not sure." He trudged through the snow with her beside him towards the lake. They were headed off the roadside together as he hugged Paige and they braced against the wind and swirling snow. This was definitely not the way he'd planned his Saturday night, but he was glad he was there for her.

As they came close to the lakeside, they paused.

"Oh, no!" she cried out.

Chapter 7

"It's going to be okay," Carter said as the wind howled around them. He wore his gloves but his hands felt frozen.

"Charlie!" Paige called out.

Instinctively, he hugged her, trying to make it all right.

Charlie was moving subtly, but he was on the ice and one move and he could fall through right it.

"Just stay calm," he soothed. "I'm going out there after him," he said, trying to calm the situation as much as possible.

"But...but what about the ice?" she said, a look of horror on her face. "You might fall through it."

"I'll be fine," he said, reassuring her. "I've just got to get to him."

He remembered this training from the military. It was time to kick into survival mode.

He inched closer to the icy snow-covered lake.

He could do this. He would get Charlie back to safety.

When he looked around, Paige's brows furrowed with panic. He could tell she was worried for Charlie and him, but he had to let her know it would be okay.

He hugged her again, giving her reassurance.

Carter figured the dept of the lake would be about five feet. He was six feet two inches, so he didn't worry about that. Or should he be worried?

What if he was wrong? What if the lake was deeper than five feet? Still, he couldn't worry about that now. He had to focus.

Get Charlie off the ice and back to safety.

He was concerned for the husky on the ice. He wondered how he even got there.

As if Paige read his mind, she said, "I left him with my friend Daphne so that I could pick up supplies but he probably got worried and came looking for me. He's supposed to take part in the sleigh ride for the kids." Guilt echoed from her voice.

"It's not your fault, Paige. He's going to be right back in your arms soon."

He did his best to reassure her. She'd had her share of loss. And he wished he could make it all better for her.

There was no way they were going to lose Charlie.

They?

He caught himself realizing *they* were no longer a couple. Not anymore. And besides, he wasn't going to get into another serious relationship ever again. He'd be the only son of his mother to not walk down the aisle. And that was that.

Carter lay flat on the ground by the bank and called to Charlie with the rope and leash in hand.

"Come here, boy. Come here, Charlie," he called out as Paige watched from the side.

Carter moved closer as safely possible.

Charlie was instinctive and probably knew he was in trouble there on the ice.

Before long, Carter slid out on the ice, the sound of cracking could be heard.

"Be careful!" Paige called out in a panic.

But Carter had to focus. One step at time. He could do this. Charlie was going to be safe on the shoreline soon.

"Charlie. Come here, boy."

The cracking became louder.

"Oh, no!" Paige called out. She rushed toward the bank.

"Stay back, Paige." He called out, worried about her safety. "We're all right."

"Are you sure? I want to be there."

"No. Too much pressure on the ice and we could all fall through. I'm good. Just hold on to the rope."

And she did while Carter inched closer and closer to Charlie.

Another heavy gust of wind and icy snow pushed over them.

He silently prayed to the man upstairs to guide him, as he'd always done. Whenever things seemed to tough or beyond his control, like the snowstorm, he had no other choice.

He had to save Charlie and he wanted to make sure Paige was all right.

"Charlie, it's all right, buddy. I'm here," Carter called out to the husky.

Carter slid carefully, inching closer to the husky. Then...

The ice cracked.

Chapter 8

"Oh, no! Carter! Are you all right?" Paige called out helplessly. Her visibility decreased with the heavy gusts of swirling snow and ice pellets made it difficult to see. But her hearing was sharp as a tool in the shed.

She heard that ice crack.

"Carter!" she called out again but heard nothing.

Guilt and torment tore through her body. It was all her fault. She'd never forgive herself if something ever happened to Carter. Charlie was her dog. And Carter was risking his life to save her dog.

She inched closer holding on tightly to the other end of the rope in her hand, just as he'd told her to do.

But the heavy gusts of wind pushed her back, ice pellets stabbing at her skin. She felt the crushing cold coming to her from all directions. She didn't wear her heavy winter coat today, since she didn't know she was going to be outside for long. That was her first mistake.

She always got hot in her heavy coat since her car was warm and every store she went into had the heat blasted on high. But now, she regretted not wearing that thicker coat.

Frost inched closer around her, suffocating her. She was sure hypothermia would get her soon. She had to stay calm. Shivering inside her coat, she wondered how long it would take her to freeze. Right now, she had to clear her mind.

She had to get to Carter and Charlie. She had to do something.

She'd underestimated this cowboy. His heart was always in the right place. Carter had always been the one she wanted to spend the rest of her life with. But she knew that if he knew the truth about her, he might just change his mind.

Let that be his decision. Tell him. A voice swept into her mind. Her heart was telling her one thing, but her mind was telling her something else.

She thought Carter would walk away when he found out, but right now, she could see he was a man up for any challenge, so what was she worried about? Rejection? Was that it? She'd been rejected by her own biological father. He left her mother when she was young. Luckily, her mother found love, a wonderful man, the man who later became Paige's father. There were good men in this world. And Carter was one of them. So why did she walk away from their engagement?

Well, one thing was for sure. She wasn't going to walk away from him now.

"Carter!" she called out again as she took one step further, hoping, praying they'd all make it out of there safely.

As Paige forced her way closer to the lake in the dark icy night, another gust of wind blew over her. She stumbled and fell hard. Pain shot through her right knee. Then...

The rope slid through her gloved hands.

Oh, no.

It's over.

There was no way she and Carter and Charlie would make it out of there now.

A chill slid through her body. Her pulse pounded hard in her throat.

Then, she heard crunching footsteps towards her and a hand on her shoulder.

"Paige?"

She looked up, snow blowing into her eyes, blocking her vision. When she squinted to see who it was, her heart leaped in her chest.

Then...

She passed out.

Chapter 9

"Paige?" Carter called out again, with the husky in his arms.

He laid Charlie down on the ground. He would wrap him in a warm blanket soon. Then he went over to Paige's side.

He didn't want to lose her. He couldn't lose her now.

Two Christmases ago, he thought she'd be his loving wife. They'd planned to have a family together. Maybe a boy and a girl if it was the Lord's will. They were going to enjoy the season, going horseback riding, ice skating, building a snowman together. But all those dreams evaporated when she broke off their engagement and told him though she loved him, they could never be together. But why? Was someone blackmailing her? Was she in trouble? Why wouldn't she tell him the real reason? She must have known he'd always be there for her.

Even if they couldn't be together, he didn't want to see any harm come to her. He still had feelings for her. His old man once told him, love never died. Well, not true love anyway.

Right now, a wave of terror surged through him, thinking she was gone.

"Paige," he said, moving closer to her. She was freezing. He had to get her warm soon. To his truck.

He lifted her up and trudged up the snowy pathway to his truck and got her inside. He wrapped a warm blanket around her. She started to shake her head and moan.

"It's okay, Paige. I'm right here with you." He turned up the heat in the pick-up, then he rushed back to Charlie's side and carried the husky into the truck.

He wrapped a blanket around Charlie too.

"What...what's happening," Paige mumbled softly.

"It's okay, darling. You just passed out there in the cold. I'm here with you now. You're going to be all right."

Darling?

Did he just call Paige darling? Again?

Just like he did when they were together? He sure hoped not. The last thing he wanted to do was to mess around with her head or to give her the wrong ideas. They were over. That's sit. Finished. There was no going back now. He wasn't doing the marriage thing anymore. And he hoped she didn't hear what he just said.

"Thank the Lord you're all right," he whispered.

Later, they ended up parked in front of her friend's house.

He didn't want to leave them alone.

"Where are we?"

"Outside your friend's house. How are you feeling?"

"Never better," she joked.

He grinned. Her humor was back.

"By the way, I called the vet," he said. "They still don't have their power back on. But Charlie's going to be good. We just need to keep him warm right now."

"Thank you," she said, softly. She turned to him.

They both leaned into each other as if magically drawn by a magnet.

Was she going to kiss him?

He inched closer to her then...

He pulled away.

"Let's get Charlie inside."

Her color had come back from the cold, but right now, she looked as if she had more color in her cheeks.

He really didn't want to hurt her feelings or mislead her, but he also couldn't lead her on. They were over. She wanted them to be apart and well, they were apart now. He couldn't do this again. It would crush his soul if she left him again. And she still didn't give him the reason why. It was better for the both of them, that they kept apart.

He wondered what was on her mind now.

What must she be thinking of him right now?

Chapter 10

He didn't kiss me.

A wave of disappointment coursed through Paige's veins. Should Paige ask him why he pulled away? No. What was she thinking? Her stomach tightened into knots. Confusion swept through her.

Who could blame him?

After all, it was Paige who broke it off with Carter.

Still, she felt a little feather of hope tickling her inside, making her feel maybe they could work this out, maybe he'd understand about her. She thought there was something there.

Maybe it was for the best that their lips didn't meet as she'd wanted. The memory of his sweet lips touching hers when they first kissed years ago still lingered inside her heart.

But a kiss would probably bring them back to a place neither wanted to be.

It would only make things hard, right?

Still, she was going to place her pride on the shelf and check her ego at the door. She had more important things to think about. Like Charlie's wellbeing. And thank heavens Carter was there to save her beloved dog.

Carter. Carter. Carter.

Why was he filling her mind and dominating her thoughts?

Because she never stopped loving him. Even after she ended their engagement. She wondered now if she'd made a wrong move.

But it was all too late now. That was in the past. And the past should stay in the past.

Oh, this is so not nice.

There was a long awkward silence that lingered in the air between them as the heavy snow fall showed no sign of ever letting up.

"We'd better get this little guy inside." Carter's voice was both authoritative and warm. She always liked that about this cowboy.

Carter got out of the truck. He paused for a moment. "You okay? How are you feeling right now?"

"Much better, thanks. I'm a lot warmer. I can feel my hands now." But what she couldn't feel was her heart, but she wasn't going to say that.

Just like the secret that she had buried in her heart, to protect both of them from heartbreak. She was going to keep that secret buried forever.

She wanted to get Charlie inside more than ever. She got out of the truck and watched as Carter opened the back door and reached inside lovingly for Charlie as if Charlie was his son. He cuddled the puffy coat soggy dog into his arms with the blanket wrapped around him.

There was something about a cowboy lovingly holding a dog to his chest that pulled at Paige's heartstrings. She wished they were a family. But she knew that was a wish that could never come true now. And probably never *should* come true.

She stroked Charlie's head as they walked up to the pathway to Daphne's home. She knew her friend would be frantic worrying about Charlie too, especially since he managed to take off from her home.

Paige was glad Carter was there for her and Charlie. He took charge of the situation despite the horrible weather conditions.

"Thank you again, Carter."

"For what?"

"For everything. For saving us." She swallowed hard, her blood pounded through her veins. "Are *you* okay? How are you feeling right now?" She held one hand to Carter's back and the other holding onto Charlie's head as they continued up the snow-filled pathway to the house.

She really wanted to know why he repelled her earlier. But she wanted to know if he was okay. Physically and emotionally.

Even though they were no longer together as a couple, Paige still wanted things to be cool between them, not *cold*.

Carter's lips thinned into a straight line, then he sighed as if he was going to speak, but then he said nothing.

She saw a glitter of hurt in his lovely ocean blue eyes.

"I'm okay, as long as you guys are," he finally said.

She knew he meant what he said.

But what else was he thinking?

Chapter 11

"Oh my goodness, are you all okay?" Daphne asked as Paige walked up the steps to her house. "I was just about to call for help. I couldn't reach you. Your cell phone kept going straight to voice mail." Daphne stood on the porch with her hands held out, ready to hug her friend.

"Yes, I'm okay." Paige could hear fatigue in her own voice from fighting the storm and her feelings for Carter.

"Come in," Daphne ushered Paige inside.

The heavy gusts of wind blew right around them and passed into the house.

"I panicked when I couldn't reach you by phone," Daphne said.

"Sorry about that," Paige said. "My battery was dead. The one in my car *and* my phone."

Daphne looked over Paige's shoulder and obviously saw a tall broad-shouldered handsome cowboy standing behind Paige holding Charlie in his arms.

"Carter?" Daphne said.

"Yes, ma'am."

"You found Charlie?" Daphne asked, looking at the pooch in the cowboy's arms.

"Sure did."

"Thank the Lord!" Daphne clasped her hands to her chest.

"It's so nice to see you again, Carter," Daphne said with enthusiasm.

"Likewise, Daphne." Carter tilted his cowboy hat. Just as he had done to Paige earlier. Always a man with class. In any situation.

Daphne knew what went down when Paige and Carter split two Christmases ago, but that was about it. She always hoped they'd get back together. Daphne had been on to Paige to tell Carter what she found out about herself in her home city. But Paige just couldn't. It wasn't something she wanted everyone to know about her.

Paige said, "Luckily Carter spotted me when my car broke down and gave me a hand and found Charlie."

"Is he going to be all right? Should he go to the vet?" Daphne said, leading them into the living room.

"Vet's down right now," Carter said. "No power."

"Still? Oh, no. Looks like not everyone's going get their power back tonight. Luckily we have ours on around here. I'm going to crank up the heat. You guys want some tea?"

"That would be great, thanks."

"Thanks," Carter said as he lay Charlie on the sofa covered with the warm blanket.

Daphne came back right away with some warm fluffy towels and dry blankets for them. Perfect for the situation.

"Daphne, you're a life saver." Paige meant it.

"Hey, no problem. I'll go look after some tea now." She left them alone.

"You should get out of those wet clothes." Paige was concerned that Carter would catch a cold. He was always the one to think of others in a crisis, but what about himself? She wanted to be the one to take care of him too.

He peeled off his wet jacket and hung it up over by the side on the coat rack. He rushed back to Charlie's side. "I'll be fine. I'm heading home soon. Besides, the jacket's waterproof. I'm dry inside. Unlike Charlie's fur." He grinned.

Paige couldn't help but catch Carter's infectious grin.

For a moment, their eyes locked and she thought he was going to mellow out. He then turned his attention back to Charlie, rubbing the dog and drying him off with the towel Daphne provided earlier.

After Charlie was dry, Carter wrapped the dog in a warm dry blanket.

"You okay, buddy?" Carter asked the dog.

Charlie barked.

Paige was joyful to hear the sounds of barking.

"He seems like he's going to be all right. I can't thank you enough Carter."

"Hey, it's no problem." He turned to face her briefly as she huddled with a blanket. She'd taken off her coat earlier when they first arrived. She shivered slightly. It was going to take her some time to warm up.

"Are you all right?" Concerned slid into Carter's voice.

"Yes, you know me. I get cold easily. Got to get my core temperature back up now."

"Make sure you drink a lot of hot fluids and get some rest too."

"Yes, sir, Doc," she teased him playfully.

His sweet lips almost curved into a smile, but then his expression turned serious and he tended to Charlie.

Daphne came back with a tray of warm gingerbread cookies and two cups of tea.,

"Aren't you having any?" Paige asked.

"Oh, I have some Christmas cards to write up. I'll leave you two alone."

That was sweet of her friend to do that. Daphne always thought about others.

Paige always admired her friend. She had a heart of gold. It was too bad Daphne's ex didn't appreciate her. He left her for some model in New York. Paige hoped Daphne would find a man to appreciate her.

Like Carter appreciated me.

After Carter finished towel drying Charlie again. He wrapped the husky in another warm dry blanket.

"What should we do now?" Paige asked eagerly, reaching over to rub Charlie's back. She'd never been in this situation before. She wondered if caring for a hypothermic dog was the same as caring for a human suffering hypothermia. Dogs had their thick coat of fur, but still, they could suffer the same fate as humans if they weren't careful.

"We've got to keep his core body temperature," Carter said, making sure Charlie was nice and cozy on the sofa. "Right now, a warm blanket and rest will do him good."

Charlie looked comfortable as he snuggled on the couch.

Her heart felt a wave of relief.

Thank you, Lord.

She was thankful that Carter was there when they needed him. What would have happened to her if he wasn't there at the right time?

It looked as if the Lord answered her silent prayers on the road tonight as always. Sending help at the right time.

"Will he be all right?" Paige asked, sipping her hot tea to try to get warm inside. Right now, she felt a chill from the icy conditions they'd been in.

"We just have to look out for signs of hypothermia. If he keeps shivering, or seems drowsy or exhausted, make sure he gets to the vet—as soon as they re-open."

"Will do." She placed her cup down and stroked Charlie's fur again.

"Try to get Charlie to drink warm liquids."

"Of course. He's so brave. Just like you."

Carter looked up at Paige as if he wanted to say something, but then he politely nodded and got up. "Listen, I'd better get back to the ranch."

"Are you sure?"

"Yes. It's better. Listen, just call me if you have any concerns."

Concerns? About Charlie? Or about us?

"Sure. And Carter, thanks so much again for everything. You really should rest a bit. I mean..."

Carter finished drinking his tea then placed the cup down.

How on earth could he drink hot tea so fast?

"Take care of yourself, Paige." He looked towards the stairs. "Please tell Daphne bye for me."

"Sure." She swallowed hard. Her stomach twisted into knots.

She wanted to keep him there. Talk to him about what really happened. For some reason, she felt he just might understand. But then another thought slid into her mind.

What if he didn't understand and she made things worse between them? Not that anything could be worse than leaving him.

With those words he put on his cowboy hat and grabbed his jacket to leave.

She was going to miss him.

Could she say anything to keep him from leaving her?

***

The look on Daphne's face said it all when she came back downstairs. Paige knew Daphne left her alone with Carter because she was hoping they would talk.

"Where is he?"

"Charlie?" Paige feigned innocent.

"No, silly," she teased. "Carter? I thought you two were going to make up."

"We're not there yet. We can't."

"You didn't tell him?"

"No. I just can't. Maybe it's for the best he left tonight. He had to go back to the ranch. Make sure all the horses are all right and his family, of course."

Carter came from a big family. He had eight brothers and several cousins on the ranch. The Charmings were a huge family. But she'd heard that his mother was concerned the family tree wasn't growing fast enough, because all the brothers were single at the moment. Could you imagine that?

Eight handsome, single cowboys on the ranch. And that did not include his cousins. Of course, in her heart Carter was stunning above the rest.

So why did she leave him then?

Earlier, she'd watch with sadness as he drove off on the snowy road. He was gone. Again. When would she ever see him again?

Should she tell him her secret?

Would he understand?

Later, after Paige had changed, she went downstairs to the kitchen where her friend was busy making a late dinner.

The staircase was beautifully decorated with holiday garlands and sparkling lights. Daphne's entire house resembled a Christmas wonderland.

Why couldn't it feel Christmas every single day of the year?

Paige remembered how she and Carter used to always ask that question.

Christmas was so romantic and heartwarming when they were together.

They used to travel around Mistletoe to the Children's Hospital, then to the shelters, dropping off presents like Mr. and Mrs. Santa Clause to all the deserving children. They'd even signed up to be Mr. and Mrs. Santa Clause two years in a row.

The expressions of hope on the faces of those they visited would forever remain in her heart. She and Carter made a great couple. Too bad she found out something that would tear them apart forever.

"Earth to Paige, paging Paige..." Daphne's voice interrupted Paige's daydream.

"Sorry," Paige said, sitting in the kitchen. "Guess I was daydreaming."

"About?"

"Nothing."

"Yeah, right. I saw the way you looked at Carter and the way he looked at you, tonight."

"What do you mean?"

"Love is blind, but the neighbors aren't," she teased. "So, are you ever going to tell Carter?"

"No."

"No? Why not? What do you think is going to happen?" Daphne looked disappointed. But not half as disappointed as Paige *felt* right now.

She hadn't expected to see Carter—not after she broke his heart unintentionally years ago—just around the holidays too. And wasn't that a coincidence that he was there when she needed help—around the holidays?

Was the Lord giving her a sign?

Should she tell Carter the truth about why she really broke up with him?

Or should she leave it be?

Lord, please guide me now. I need you. I'm so torn, I don't know what to do.

"So why don't you tell Carter the truth?" Daphne arched a brow.

"Because..."

"Because what? You think he wouldn't understand?"

"I think he'd never want to be around me. And I think it would hurt him if he found out. And the last thing I want to do is hurt him."

"Don't you think you're hurting him now?"

Chapter 12

Did she meet someone else?

Was that it?

The thoughts raced through Carter's mind the following week when he drove to the feed store to pick up some supplies. As the snow fell hard, he couldn't help but think about Paige.

The town of Mistletoe was blanketed in a coat of white all around. It would have been perfect if Paige and he were still a couple. She'd always loved the snow fall. She told him she wanted to get married at Christmas. And he could think of no other better time. They'd had so much fun during the winter season in Mistletoe. They used to go caroling then later have snowball fights and then take part in all the other fun festivities. But then she left him. Just like that.

Now Paige was back?

He wondered what she was really there for.

He wished the Lord would give him a sign and tell him what this was about. He'd been hurt before and his heart was under lockdown so what was this about?

He'd been so busy this week with fixing up the ranch for Christmas along with his brothers, trying to forget about her and what she'd done to him, but it wasn't helping.

Last week, when his mother had asked him who was stuck out there in the snowbank with their blinkers on, he'd told her it was a lady, but he didn't say anything more. He didn't want to open up any more wounds or get anyone's hopes up. His mother loved Paige and was just as confused as he was when she left him like that.

The door chime made a jingle bell sound as Carter walked into the feed store.

"Hey there," Jim, the owner of the store, called out.

"Hey there yourself." Carter's tone was friendly. "What's going on?"

The place was covered in festive lights and decorations. Jim, she feed store owner, was all ready for the Christmas season. Gave everyone who walked in a warm and cozy feeling. But right now, Carter wished he could feel warm and cozy. It always brought back memories of him and Paige when they went Christmas shopping together or gathering supplies around the holiday season.

"That's what I was about to ask you," Jim said. "Guess who's in town?"

Old man Jim was a nice guy but he did love to gossip. That's what happened in a small town. Everybody knew everything going on and everybody's business.

Carter admired Jim and his wife Marva. They ran the feed store together and have been married for over 50 years!

Carter wondered if he'd ever find happiness with a wife of his own one day. But then he realized maybe marriage wasn't for everyone.

"Who?" Carter asked, he didn't want to be too presumptuous. After all, the town didn't revolve around him.

"Paige. I saw her this morning. She's back in town." Jim's eyes were hopeful.

Carter could tell Jim was hoping that he and Paige would get back together. When she left town she'd told everyone she wasn't coming back. Made it look as if Carter did something to her and she didn't want to be near him.

Jim knew that Carter had planned this special big wedding with Paige until she up and left him and broke off the engagement. The wave of humiliation still stayed with him but not as much as his broken heart. He couldn't let Paige near his heart again. Never again. And right now, he felt something for her, but he had to ignore it. He had to dismiss that spark of attraction he had to beautiful Paige last week during the snow blackout. He had to ignore that tingling sensation he felt when their hands brushed again in his truck.

Last week, he'd arranged for his friend to tow her car and he'd paid for it, because that's what a cowboy did. But when he saw her calling back, he couldn't answer the call. Not just yet. He let it go to voicemail.

What was he afraid of?

He was afraid of falling for her again and having his heart ripped out of his chest and shredded into tiny confetti pieces. He just couldn't go there. As much as he still had feelings for her, it was probably best they stay apart.

Chapter 13

The following week, Paige attended the spectacular tree lighting ceremony at the Town Square.

Later, she and Daphne visited the grounds of the Children's Hospital. They all stood outside in the cold but her heart melted with warmth when she saw how much the children enjoyed the fun yet functional design of the new play area.

For the Christmas theme, there was a magical mini winter wonderland theme park near the hospital, complete with Santa's workshops and elves, played by volunteers.

Still, her mind was on Carter.

Last week, she tried to thank him for getting her car fixed and of course, saving Charlie's life and hers. But he just wouldn't see her.

Daphne had told Paige earlier that Carter had been acting funny over the holidays since Paige left town. He rarely came out for the town's celebrations.

"Are you all right?" Daphne asked.

"Oh, yes, of course."

"Do you think he's ready?"

"No, I don't think he's ready to talk. I tried to have a conversation about the past, but..."

"Uh, sorry, girl. I'm talking about Charlie. Do you think he's ready to do the sleigh ride with the kids outside?"

A wave of heat rushed through Paige just then. Heat of embarrassment. "Yes, of course, that's what you're talking about," Paige chuckled nervously. "Yes, he's ready."

Charlie was outside getting warmed up for the fun dog sleigh ride for some of the kids who were well enough to participate,.

Charlie loved being around kids and it appeared the feeling was mutual.

"Let's go," Paige said, trying to ignore the concerned look on her friend's face.

The truth was, Paige was miserable without Carter.

This was different from the last time. This time, she was reminded about how much she loved him. She was reminded about how caring he was, especially around her new dog. Her dog in crisis. He really stepped up to the plate. He knew exactly what to do and how to do it and he was so nurturing.

Daphne and Paige walked around with some of the volunteers from the hospital. The sound of Christmas music and laughter filled the air.

She wondered what Carter was doing right now.

Maybe, he would be okay with her secret.

Or maybe not.

Just then, her heart stopped when she saw a gorgeous cowboy nearby.

It was Carter.

He looked stunning wearing a red jacket and matching pants with cowboy hat. Was he helping out with the Christmas Day festivities at the hospital?

She could see the side glance expression from her friend, Daphne. But she tried to ignore it and focus on Carter.

"Hi, ladies," he said in a warm voice, tilting his cowboy hat as he approached them.

"Hi, there." Butterflies exploded in Paige's stomach.

"Hi," Daphne said.

Paige wondered if he felt guilty for ignoring this past week since the storm.

"I see you're participating in the Christmas Day," Paige said.

"Yeah, it's just a little support for Santa, when he arrives."

"You're not an elf?"

He chuckled. "Nope. Too tall for that. Last year, Santa's sleigh got stuck and we had to help him out as the kids rushed over to him. Almost toppled the sleight with presents. It was quite a sight."

"I can imagine." She knew Carter was good with kids and she was glad he was helping out although Daphne told her that Carter had vanished from participating in all the adult Christmas celebrations since Paige left him. Including the festive annual barn dance.

She shuddered thinking that she could be responsible for him not enjoying Christmas. Come to think of it, she'd broken up with him over the Christmas holidays, so who could blame him?

If she could do it all over again, she would have waited until the new year. But then again, it looked as if there was no good time to break up with the one you love.

Daphne's phone rang and she excused herself to take the call and walked away leaving Paige and Carter alone.

"Are you enjoying yourself?" he asked.

"Yes, I am. You?"

Okay, enough small talk. Was he trying to ask her something? Was he going to ask her to the annual Christmas barn dance?

She would absolutely love to go with him.

"Listen, I just wanted to apologize for not getting back to you sooner," he said.

"It's no problem. I get it. You're busy. It's a busy time of the year. And...I want to thank you again for saving Charlie."

"No problem. Anything for...for Charlie. And I'm glad you're okay as well." He looked over at the sound of cheers and screams of joy as Charlie pulled the kids on the sleigh."

"Looks like Charlie is the one doing the saving," Carter said. "He's saving the day for the kids."

"He sure is."

Was he going to ask her to the dance? Were they going to get a chance to kiss under the town's famous mistletoe?

"There's something I need to tell you." They both spoke in unison and Paige laughed, Carter grinned.

It was like old times, only it wasn't. Something was different this time around. And they both knew it.

"What were you going to say?" he asked, his voice was soft and gentle like the pretty snowflakes falling gently.

Should she tell him now?

No. Now was not a good time, of course. But she was going to tell him that they needed to talk about what happened when she went back to Texas.

She had a sudden overwhelming feeling to come clean with Carter. And maybe, just maybe start over again. Or was she overthinking things?

"Carter, I..."

Just then, a loud noise sounded. And the kids all screamed for joy. It was Santa Clause arriving with presents.

"Sorry, what were you going to say?" he asked.

"Oh, nothing. You go on ahead. I'll catch up with you later."

"You sure?"

"Yes, I'm sure."

She wasn't sure. But what she was sure about was she should leave Mistletoe and head back to Texas. She was exploring the idea of working as an interior designer for a new facility there. Maybe it was all the spirit of the season why she though it would be a good idea to come clean with Carter, but now she knew better.

She would leave things be. As soon as Charlie finished his sleigh-ride fun, they would be heading back to Texas.

***

"So, what are you going to do now?" Daphne asked Paige after the Christmas festivities at the Children's Hospital.

Paige and Daphne walked through the marketplace towards Daphne's home after the event. They each gave Charlie a huge hug after the kids got a chance to hug him and thank him for the fun sleigh ride. It was quite an experience.

"I'm heading home."

"Now?" Daphne asked, incredulously.

"No, after Christmas, of course. It would be nice for Charlie to experience the fun vibe of Mistletoe at Christmas."

"And what about you?"

"Well," Paige sighed. "I think I should keep as far away as possible from Carter. I've hurt him enough in the past and he saved Charlie's life."

"So, you're not going to tell him the real reason you broke off your engagement?"

"Does it matter? He's probably moving on now. Every time I try to get close to him, he pulls away. And who could blame him?"

"I was looking forward to seeing you two at the barn dance, you know, kissing under the mistletoe."

"It looks like there won't be a cowboy under the mistletoe for me this Christmas," Paige chuckled, trying to hide the hurt swelling up inside her.

Just then...

Paige paused. It was Carter again, in his Christmas suit and cowboy hat. He looked so charming and delightful.

"Hey," he said. Obviously still buzzing from all the excitement of the day.

"Hey," Paige said. Daphne quickly slipped away pretending to look at some ornaments from a market stall.

"Surprised to see Santa's helper here," Paige said with a smile.

"Listen, I forgot to invite you to the annual Christmas Barn Dance."

"Really?" Her heart galloped in her chest.

She wanted to say, she thought he stopped attending Christmas events.

"So, you want me to be your date?" she asked hopefully.

"Actually, I won't be attending, but I want you and Charlie to be there. Have some fun. The family would love to see you. Mom's always asking about you."

Her stomach tightened into knots.

"Of course," she said, trying to hide her disappointment. Well, for one thing, she was glad his family didn't hate her after she left him. They had all gotten along in the past. She always thought they'd make the perfect in-laws. They were down to earth and so caring, just like Carter.

"Good. I'll let my family know you'll be there."

She was about to ask him why he won't be attending when another helper called out to him.

"Hey, cowboy! You're wanted for more photos."

She could see kids huddling around the Santa's lap area grabbing at toys and some taking pictures with Santa and his helpers.

"Sorry, I have to go, but I hope you enjoy yourself."

He touched her arm and she tingled inside.

"I will." *Not. Especially knowing you won't be there.*

He left and went over to the corner, his tall frame moving through the crowds. He then leaned down and picked up one of the kids who clapped and squealed with excitement.

It was then that Paige knew Carter would make a great dad someday.

"Are you okay?" Daphne returned with a bag full of ornaments.

"No," Paige whispered. "I don't know if I'll ever be okay."

"What happened? What did he say?"

"He invited me to the barn dance."

"Great! And you're upset because...?"

"I'm going alone."

"Oh, not so great."

"Yes. You're right, he doesn't do adult holiday activities, not anymore."

"So what are you going to do?" Daphne placed her free hand on her hip and gave Paige that mischievous look.

Oh, no. She had an idea what was on Daphne's mind.

Chapter 14

Carter's heart pumped hard in his chest as he made his way to his truck. He placed the sack of tools in the back of his pickup after his volunteer gig at the hospital.

His mind was still on Paige.

He was always mesmerized by her beauty, her charm, her aura. Even though she left him high and dry right before their wedding.

He wanted to turn back right now and go back to the market. He wanted to hug her, to kiss her again, just like old times.

But these weren't old times. This was the new reality. Paige and he were still apart.

He really wanted to take Paige to the dance, but he didn't want to send her mixed signals. It was over between them. She wanted nothing to do with him so he had to respect that.

He took off his helper jacket and left it in the back seat. Then he slammed the door shut and adjusted his cowboy hat.

He was going to see her again. He felt in his heart that she had something to tell him. He wanted to at least hear her out.

Later, when he returned to the marketplace, she was nowhere in sight.

He'd missed his chance. Cinderella had already left the ball. And there was no trace of a glass slipper anywhere.

"Hey bro," Noel's voice sounded beside him.

"Hey, yourself," Carter replied, still looking around, trying to pick Paige out in the crowd of people and the sound of the loud Christmas music playing over the sound speakers.

"You look like you lost something."

"I did. Paige was here."

"Right. I didn't want to say anything, but I met up with her just now."

"You did?" Carter was surprised. How did his little bro see her and he didn't.

"Yeah, she said she was going back to Texas. Her pooch had fun helping out and it was time to go back. Think she has some job lined up there. She was on her cell phone when I saw her."

"Oh, no."

"What's wrong?"

"Nothing."

Paige was leaving Mistletoe and heading back to Texas?

This was a disaster. Why wouldn't she even stick around till Christmas? Her parents were now with the Lord. She mentioned something about spending time here so she wouldn't be alone.

He felt alone right now.

Just then, Noel saw a friend and patted Carter on the back, telling him he'd see him later.

Oh, Paige.

Paige was the only thing on his mind right now.

The truth was, he felt so alive when she was around him for those moments in the storm and back at Daphne's house until he left them. She always made him feel that way, whether in a dangerous situation like the storm or at home inside.

Had Carter driven her away for good by being distant this past week? Was it something he said or did or was it his unintentional emotional distancing? He'd learned that when he was in foster care before he was adopted by the Charming family—he tended to distance himself from those around him.

He'd been so aloof with Paige when she returned to Mistletoe. Not wanting to send mixed signals or get his heart crushed again. But now, he understood that when he told her he wouldn't actually be attending the barn dance, she probably took that as a sign that he didn't want to see her again.

He reached into his pocket and pulled out his cell phone

How was he going to make this right?

It was too late. She was gone.

Chapter 15

The Christmas music was alive at the barn hall. The choir sang *O Come, All Ye Faithful* with an upbeat tempo. The sounds of laughter, singing and chatter filled the decorative barn.

The beautiful decorations and lights lit up the place. You would never know it was a renovated barn. It always had the cozy festive feel to it.

"Carter! You're here!" his mother went over to him and hugged him. "Well, this is the first in a long time."

"I thought you said you weren't coming, bro," Evan, his brother, said with a glass of eggnog in his hand.

"I changed my mind," Carter said. "I said, why not?"

The truth was he didn't want to be alone tonight.

"You have to kiss under the mistletoe, it's good luck. Your daddy and I did once and we married and were happy every day of our marriage."

He gave his mother a grin and playfully rolled his eyes. Seriously? Did his mother expect him to just kiss any girl under the mistletoe?

He wanted Paige. But the truth was, he couldn't have her. Not anymore.

Paige hadn't answered any of his calls. He worried about her, wondering if she was all right. Travelling back to Texas in this weather alone got him all concerned.

When he'd driven by Daphne's house there was no one there.

He thought that was odd.

Paige was really gone, wasn't she?

And he had a chance to reach out to her but he didn't. She wanted to explain why she left him but he didn't or couldn't hear it at the time.

"Well, look who's here," said a jovial voice behind him. It was Sister Sue Ellen from the church.

Oh, no. That meant her niece was probably nearby. He knew his family was trying to set him up with Peggy Sue, but he just wasn't interested in seeing anyone.

Well, up until tonight. He wasn't interest in seeing anyone except Paige. But that was now out of the question.

"Hello, Sister Sue." Carter was careful to call her by her preferred pet name.

She hugged his arm and led him towards the other side of the barn. "I have someone you need to meet," she said, a wide loving smile on her face.

She was a charming older lady and he always had respect and nothing but love for all the church sisters. They were all like aunties to him and his brothers. It was a close-knit community in Mistletoe, especially at the church.

He could see from the corner of his eyes, his brothers Noel and Evan sharing glances then grinning. His mother gave a nod of approval as he walked with Sister Sue.

When he stood in front of Peggy Sue, she glanced up at him and yawned. She was in her forties and recently divorced. She always had a thing for corporate guys. She wasn't too much into cowboys. She went to a finishing school in Sweden when she was younger.

They didn't have much in common and he was certain she felt the same way.

But in the spirit of the season and during this family occasion, he thought there was no harm in having dance.

He took of his cowboy hat and greeted her. She nodded and sighed as if she wished she could be anywhere but there. He felt the same way, but he wasn't going to say anything.

"I'll leave you two alone," Sister Sue said as she walked away, her head held up high and a mischievous grin on her lips.

"I'm sorry about this," Peggy said. My mother feels as if there must be something wrong with me since I'm not remarried.

"Hey, it's no trouble at all. My folks, well, my mother feels the same way. Let's say we make the best of the moment. And at least have that dance."

"You mean the dance and that mistletoe kiss?" she said, rolling her eyes. "I'm sorry, no offence, but I don't feel like being the new couple under the mistletoe this year."

"No offence taken. You want to dance?"

"Now *that* I can do." She placed her glass of eggnog down and place her hand into the crook of his arm. He led her to the dance floor. He was a gentleman after all. He was going to show her a good time on the floor. He was already there, so why not make the most of it?

***

Paige braced herself as she stood outside the barn door leading into the hall. She could hear the sound of laughter and clapping and Christmas music coming from the barn.

"You okay?" Daphne asked Paige.

"Yes, I'm fine. The doctor said I should get the lab results any day now. Until then, I'm going to reach out to Carter. The least I could do is let him know why I left him and ask him to give us another chance. Life is too short not to go for what you want. I never should have left him."

"Well, here's your chance to set things straight, girl. So glad you're back."

Paige hugged Daphne and then she made her way into the barn by herself.

When she reached inside, she instantly spotted her handsome cowboy. But...

He was dancing with another woman.

And they seemed to be enjoying each other's company.

This was a *huge* mistake!

Was this woman going to be Carter's mistletoe kiss? She thought she'd have her cowboy under the mistletoe this Christmas. But she was wrong. The last thing she wanted to do was to make things awkward or embarrass him.

Paige turned and walked right back out of the barn.

Chapter 16

Paige stood outside the barn door, catching her breath.

It was too late.

Carter was with someone else.

She should just turn around and go back home. She came back to tell him her secret, but maybe it was for the best that she didn't have the chance.

Daphne had already driven off. Daphne had been invited earlier to the dance but didn't feel up to dancing tonight but was good enough to give Paige a ride there.

Paige pulled out her cell phone. It had about just as much battery as she had in her emotional case. She felt as if she was running on empty. Why did it feel as if the air had been squeezed out of her body?

"Paige?" A smooth deep voice sounded behind her.

She turned around.

It was Carter.

She could not hide the relief.

"Carter, I..."

"I saw you walk out of the barn."

'I didn't want to trouble you.'

"No. I'm glad you came."

"I see you have a date." She swallowed hard. She had no right to his business. *She* left him. Not the other way around. But that's not how she felt. She really wanted to know if he'd just met someone else.

"It's okay. We just met up tonight." He looked deep into her eyes. And her heart turned over in her chest. Butterflies exploded in her stomach. They were inches apart now and she felt that sweet magnetic pull between them that she'd always felt. It never went away.

The sweet scent of his cologne wafted to her nostrils with the gentle breeze.

"Are you all right?"

"No. Carter, there's something I need to tell you."

"What it is?" His voice was soft and calm.

"The real reason I left you was..." She sucked in a deep breath in the cold air. "I didn't want you to get hurt."

There, she said it.

"Hurt? How could you hurt me?"

"The same way my mother inadvertently hurt my father. She hadn't told him she had a rare congenital heart disorder—something that's been passed down to my genes."

"Oh, no. I'm so sorry to hear that, honey."

He called her honey. She always loved when he called her that.

"It's okay. I knew you were devasted with the loss of your own father, And I watched as my father was demolished when my mother passed and it tore his heart apart during the time he cared her for up until her passing. I couldn't bring myself to let you go through what Dad went through with Mom."

"Gosh, Paige. You have no idea how much I'm torn about what happened to your parents. But I would never leave you. I care about you. All of you. I care about your condition, and I care more about you. My life hasn't been the same without you. I want to take care of you, to stand beside you, behind you, every step of the way."

He bit down on his lip.

"I'll be here for you no matter what. You don't have to go through this alone. I'll be at your side. None of us can control the length of our time here only the depth of it. Being with the one you love makes the journey worthwhile."

Her heart tugged with emotion. Overcome with warm feelings, she could barely speak.

She was happy to hear that. He wanted to be with her whether for a month or a millennium.

She hugged him and felt the warmth of his touch.

"I wish you hadn't made that decision for me of whether I could live with your condition," he continued. "God can make a way where there is no way. You know that."

Her heart sank.

Of course, the man upstairs provided a way for her to get help when Charlie was lost in the storm. Look at how in charge Carter was when Charlie was lost and then he nurtured Charlie back to life. How could she have made that decision for Carter?

"Well, what do we do now?"

"I say, we get you back inside the barn and we have our dance." A warm smile played on his sweet lips. "Paige. I want to be there for you no matter what. I still want to spend the rest of my life with you, if that's what you want."

"Of course, it is. Are you okay with my...with the fact that we may not have as long as we want?" She bit down on her lip.

He looked up to the dark night sky with the soft snow flurries falling softly. Then he looked down at Paige, a sweet grin on his lips.

Was he going to kiss her?

They leaned in together, then...

The barn door flung open.

"Hey, you two, we're having the last dance of the evening," Noel called out.

They both grinned and walked back towards the barn.

Just then, Paige's phone rang. She reached into her purse to pull it out. It was the lab.

A worried expression must have surfaced on her face because Carter asked her if she as okay.

"It's the lab. They said they'd call with the recent blood results."

"I'm right here for you, Paige." He hugged her and she instantly felt relief, comfort.

When she got off the phone she stood still.

"What did they say?" he asked softly.

Tears welled in her eyes. "I'm going to be okay. I don't have the aggressive form of the gene like my mother. They said my life expectancy is going to be a lot longer—in fact it's going to be normal. Oh, praise the Lord!"

He smiled and hugged her tight.

Later, they both swayed to the music for the last dance, *Silent Night*. A blessed night and a beautiful ballad to dance to.

A bell sounded and everyone cheered for the couples to kiss under their mistletoe.

"Well, what do you say?" Carter asked Paige with a boyish sweet grin.

She tilted her head up to him and he leaned down as they met halfway and brushed their lips together in a sweet and delicious kiss. Right under the mistletoe, sealing their future together and a love to last a lifetime.

COWBOY'S CHRISTMAS BLESSING:
Rescued by the Cowboy at Christmas Book 2

(Sweet Clean Christian Western Romance)
By J. A. Somers

COWBOY'S CHRISTMAS BLESSING

Evan Charming is one cowboy who isn't looking for love again. He'd lost his wife in a tragic accident. He is determined to never fall in love again—and to never celebrate the holidays.

Gwen Cameron has a lot on her plate. Always trying to prove herself. She doesn't have a lot of luck with relationships. Her ex left her for her best friend. Still, this Christmas, after taking over her late father's tow-truck business, she decides to bury herself in her work. But meeting a tall handsome cowboy may change her plans.

Can two lost souls unite in the spirit of Christmas?

Chapter 1

"Life is a blessing. It's an adventure. You're supposed to *live* it. Isn't that what you and Rhonda used to say?" Evan Charming's brother Cameron said.

The two brothers strung up decorations around the Barn Hall at Charming Ranch for their upcoming annual Christmas celebration. The Charming's Ranch and Resort hosted Christmas for many deserving families around the holidays.

Their mother, a widow and part time matchmaker at the Mistletoe Church, always made sure to keep up the tradition their father and grandfather started many years ago.

She was especially protective of her many sons and nephews and let them know her wishes for them to be happily married—again. She wanted nothing more than to see them happy and to have the ranch filled with grandkids.

Cameron also lost his wife and stepdaughter in a fire. He'd closed himself off from doing fun things in life since then. Cameron was coming around a bit now, but he was always the encourager in the family—anything to take his mind off his own sorrow.

Evan was there for his brother back then when it had happened. It seemed like they all had only each other to rely on.

With the rows of holiday lights strung up outside and garlands inside the newly renovated barn-turned-event hall, it was supposed to put everyone in the festive mood, but right now, Evan felt anything but festive.

He was glad his other brother Noel met his match and was happily married now. But would it ever happen for Evan—again?

He knew he was blessed but sometimes he found it hard to count his blessings after Rhonda went to be with the Lord.

"I'm just not interested in any more adventures," Evan replied. "They're too dangerous."

"Says the cowboy who never passed up an opportunity to stare danger in the face."

This time of the year brought nothing but dread over Evan. He knew he should be celebrating the holidays with his family.

"It's the anniversary. You know how I feel."

Cameron's face fell. "I'm really sorry, bro. I know it must be hard on you. But I just don't want to see you lose yourself. Rhonda would have wanted you to move forward. She wouldn't want you to stop living."

"I know. I thought she was one of my biggest blessings."

"She was."

"But she's no longer with me. I feel as if I'm..."

"Don't say it, man."

"You know what I mean. I think there's one special soul mate for everyone and she was it."

"Have you tried going out on a date? What about the women's ministry?"

"No, thanks. Mom's being trying to hook me up with someone's niece."

"You too, huh?" Cameron chuckled.

He appreciated his brother trying to lift his spirits. But it was no use. His chance had come and gone. His late wife was his chance. That was it. He was determined to go it alone from this time forward. He might be one tough cowboy, but his heart couldn't take any more heartbreak.

Actually, Evan lit a candle for his late wife—every month since her passing.

It wasn't just sorrow. It was guilt. Yes, guilt that washed over him each and every single day.

Why, oh, why didn't he dissuade Rhonda from going on that mountain climb?

She was always up for a challenge. Any challenge. She was adventurous to a fault. They both were—back then. He just wished he'd been there with her at the time.

If he was, he wondered if it would have made a big difference. It seemed the Lord called her home too soon. It was way too soon for Evan.

He watched as the snow fell harder outside. Mistletoe had the most ravaging winters. But this weather also reminded him of his late wife on the mountain side. She was with other climbers at the time. None of them him.

She'd asked him to go with her, but he had business in town. Though he and his brothers lived in cabins on the massive Charming Ranch, they each had their own business endeavors. He'd spent way too much time in the office and he couldn't wait to bury himself in work.

As far as he was concerned, he didn't deserve a second chance.

"Well, we're done here," Evan said. "I'm heading back to town."

"Please tell me you're not going to the office now?" Cameron looked disappointed. "Mom's hosting the gingerbread bake-off tonight."

"I'm sorry, man. I'll call mom soon. I just need to get away from here right now."

His brother had the look on his face that he understood. Christmas time was too hard for Evan right now. He and Rhonda used to participate in all the events around this time of the year, helping out on the ranch. But not now.

He didn't know if he'd ever feel the spirit of the season again.

Was it even possible?

Chapter 2

Gwen Cameron was *not* having a good evening. She placed the chained hitch hook on the bumper of the client's car, getting ready to tow it when she heard a terrible noise coming from her own vehicle. It sounded awful. When she turned around she saw smoke coming from her own engine. Her tow truck broke down.

Oh, great.

What was she going to do now?

She was supposed to be helping a customer and now *she* needed help.

The gusty winds swirled the snow and made the visibility worse. She'd had a long day towing so many vehicles today so this was the last thing she needed.

Her father hadn't left things in a great condition. But it wasn't his fault. He'd been sick the last few months of his life.

Cameron Towing had been in her family business for decades. But after her father went to be with the lord, she was his only child, and the only one who could keep things going. There was no way she was going to let her father's business be swallowed up by the big buys.

He wanted to keep it in the family and she was going to make sure that it was kept in the family.

This wasn't exactly her line of work, though her father had showed her the ropes a few times while growing up, but she caught on quickly. Well, she caught on quickly when it came to learning new tricks of the trade, but not when it came on to knowing her best friend had helped herself to Gwen's then fiancé.

Live and learn.

She wondered if the Lord had forgotten about her. She'd hoped to be with that special someone who made her heart go pitter patter. But now the only pitter patter she heard was the sound of hale and snow on the windshield.

She turned back again to make sure her customer was all right, while she fought the bitter cold to get the broken-down vehicle secured.

Mrs. Bane was seated comfortably in the passenger side of Gwen's truck. She always made sure to take care of her clients.

Mrs. Bane was a member of the Mistletoe Church. And she had been more than caring when Gwen's dad passed away last Christmas. Mrs. Bane had brought over baked goods and soup during that time period. Always checking up on Gwen. She had told Mrs. Bane this tow was for free when she arrived on the scene. But then it looked like it wasn't even going to happen, because they were going nowhere fast.

Mrs. Bane was one of the oldest drivers in Mistletoe. At age 87, she still had remarkable energy and a quick sharp mind. Unfortunately, her little blue automobile, something she's had in her family for the longest time, wasn't as quick or sharp. And right now, Gwen was having a hard time getting it hooked up.

Gwen tried her cell phone to call for back up support from the office.

She glanced at the screen of her cell phone.

The battery was going down fast at 1%, the red bar at the top of the screen meant she needed a charger fast.

When she reached into her pockets, she realized that she didn't have her charger with her. She had a last call about an hour ago and was about to head home to recharge her phone and her own emotional battery when she got this last call from Mrs. Bane.

Mrs. Bane rolled down the window, "Are you all right, dear?" she called out.

"Mrs. Bane, I'm fine," Gwen said reassuringly. "You'd better keep the window up. It's freezing out here."

Mrs. Bane smiled and rolled the window back up.

The elder lady had been hospitalized last year for pneumonia and was prone to hypothermia as she once told the prayer group last year.

Gwen was glad to be of assistance, but it looked as if she might be running out of more than just time.

Chapter 3

Evan couldn't wait to get back to the office. There wasn't much in life he could control, such as the death of his now late wife, but there were some things he could control. His work. That's when he decided he would spend more and more time at work. Even over the holidays.

He steered his Ford Pickup down the snow-covered side road, ready to make an entrance on the main road.

The drive on the road gave him way too much time to think. He remembered when he and Rhonda drove for hours looking for the perfect Christmas tree. That was just two years ago. He had no idea that would have been the last time.

Stop that, Evan. Your brother's right. Stop obsessing over the past. It's gone. There's nothing you could ever do to bring her back.

His old man used to tell him, "You've got to live your life looking ahead not backward." And he was right.

This cowboy had to find a way to move forward, but he couldn't do it on his own.

"Oh, Lord, help me find a way to be strong again," he whispered under his breath. He used to talk to the man upstairs every day, well, his late wife used to, but those moments got less and less for him now. He knew deep down these were the times when he needed to reconnect. Right now, he needed the strength to let go of the past, the hurt, the guilt, the pain. Could he ever do that?

The silence of the night seemed to be his worst enemy right now. His thoughts raced whenever there was no noise. Maybe that's why he stayed late at the office. It was like a medication.

Being around files and reports and co-workers busying around the building.

He reached for his radio to turn it on. Maybe having sound in his truck besides the engine and the sound of his wheels grinding on the snow would be good. But the radio station played Christmas tunes 24 hours around the clock during this time of the year. His stomach lurched when he heard his late-wife's favorite Christmas song, *The First Noel*.

He loved the way his late wife had belted out the tune with her high octave vocals. It always gave him chills when she sang. His eyes stung for a moment.

He sucked in a deep breath and realized he was getting emotional. Should he switch the station? He wanted to but something urged him not to. Was it Rhonda? Was she telling him something? Was the man upstairs trying to tell him something? He wished he knew what it was.

Just then, he spotted a tow truck with blinkers on and some smoke coming from it. He saw two figures on the roadside beside a car, one of them looked like an older person. They were huddled together.

Oh, no.

His heart pumped hard and fast in his chest. He pulled over to the side, a surge of energy rushed through him.

The women looked stiff.

Was he too late?

Chapter 4

"Are you two all right?" Evan said walking closer to the two women at the side of the road.

Just then, one of them looked up. She had the most beautiful eyes he'd ever seen, but her eyes were filled with despair.

"Hi," she said, hugging the other woman.

"Hi," he said back. "What happened here?" He moved closer to them. "How can I help?"

"Thanks for offering," she said. "I'm just trying to keep her warm. Her car ended up in the snowbank there and I came to help her out."

"I see," he said, looking at the tow truck. "First let's get you two out of the cold. My pickup's nice and warm."

"Thank you. Thank you so much!" The gratitude in her voice was evident. She was humble and sweet, he could tell.

He helped the older lady up, holding on to one arm while the younger woman held onto the other.

"Oh, where am I?" the older woman said.

"Mrs. Bane, remember, your car slid into the snowbank and you called me for help."

"Oh, dear." The woman looked lost and shook her head.

Evan's heart went out to Mrs. Bane. He then realized Mrs. Bane also went to his church. She was a widow. She was married to her now late husband for over 65 years. Now, she was all alone and wanted to maintain what was left of her independence. Her life. It couldn't be easy for her. Mr. and Mrs. Bane were practically inseparable. He'd always admired that couple. He'd heard that one morning she woke up and he was gone. He went peacefully in his sleep.

Evan remembered driving his mother to the Bane's house to bring the widow some comfort and some warm pies she'd baked that day.

It was a good thing the other woman helped Mrs. Bane and got them both out of a cold vehicle.

It was dangerous, especially without some heat circulating. She did the right thing by huddling up. But what if he hadn't seen them? How long could they have kept that up? He shuddered to think about that.

This pretty lady was a tow truck operator?

He hadn't seen her before. He recognized the sign on the truck though. Maybe she was new to the company. He knew Cameron Tow Truck Service, but the old man Cam, as everyone the town called him, passed away, didn't he? Was this his daughter?

After he got the older lady in his own truck, he said, "I'm Evan Charming, by the way."

"I know," she said warmly, "I'm Gwen Cameron. Cam's daughter."

"Oh, *you're* Cam's daughter?" He eyed the beautiful woman before him with the lovely rose-colored lips and the prettiest brown eyes he'd ever seen.

Gwen.

He remembered now.

Gwen sure looked different from the last time he'd seen her. They were in elementary school and she had the biggest braids and flaming red hair. She sure looked different right now.

"I'm sorry, I didn't recognize you."

"It's okay, I've changed over the years."

Nope, she was as pretty now as she was then. Her hair looked different but that lovely oval-shaped face was still the same. He'd had a little crush on her back then. But they never kept in touch after high school. She'd moved somewhere out west. Her father carried on the shop after her mother died, so he'd heard through the small-town grapevine.

Moments later, after they'd gotten Mrs. Bane into the passenger-side seat of Evan's pickup, Gwen made some calls using Evan's cellphone since her battery died. She placed a call to Mrs. Bane's nephew to see if he could be there when they dropped Mrs. Bane home. They didn't want her to be alone on a night like tonight. She might have to see a doctor.

Right now, Evan and Gwen were on the same page. Getting Mrs. Bane to safety.

Once Mrs. Bane was inside the pickup, Evan went to survey Gwen's tow truck.

She came back to his side, her snow boots crunching in the snow.

"So, is the engine overheated?" she asked in her sweet soft voice.

He loved the sound of her voice.

Right now, this cowboy had to focus. What was he thinking? He shouldn't even be focusing on her soft sway or her lovely voice. Her tow truck and getting Gwen and Mrs. Bane to safety was the only thing on this cowboy's mind right now.

Focus, cowboy. Focus.

"It's an old engine," he said, looking under the hood. "Thankfully, it's not overheating. But you will need to get it replaced. The oil's burned."

"I see," she said, hugging herself in the chilly night.

He wished he could reach over and hug her to help her keep warm.

Evan, what's with you, man?

Stop those thoughts.

What was with him all of a sudden? Why was he having thoughts about this lovely young lady whom he went to high school with? That should be the last thing on his mind right now.

"Looks like I need to take some lessons in auto mechanic," she continued.

"It's all right. Not everyone knows that."

"I thought you were a corporate cowboy." She smiled.

"Dad taught us everything we need to know about everything," he said.

A sad feeling crept over him just now. He missed his old man. He wished his dad was still around. He always thought about his dad, especially around the holidays. His father and his mother always made it special.

He then pushed the hood of the tow truck down.

He made a call on his phone.

Later, when he'd finished he said, "I've got someone on the way with a flatbed tow. He'll be here soon to take both of your vehicles. Where can I take you ladies?"

She looked up into his eyes. For a moment, there was something there. Or maybe that was his imagination.

"Mrs. Bane's nephew said he's out of town. He can't be with her. I don't feel comfortable leaving her alone right now."

"Gotcha. I was about to say the same thing." He pulled out his cell phone again and made a call to the ranch. His mother loved Mrs. Bane and would be happy for her to stay there the night until she was all right.

"Okay, it's settled," he said.

"What is?"

"My mother would be happy to stay with Mrs. Bane, either at her home or at the ranch."

Gwen's appreciative smile was infectious. Her eyes lit up when she knew Mrs. Bane would be all right.

Just then a thought struck him. Wasn't Mrs. Bane on the Women's Ministry with his mother? She was one of church's matchmakers, wasn't she?

Oh, boy. Talk about timing.

His mother had been on him to find a match and said the Lord worked in mysterious ways.

He immediately swept the thought out of his mind. That was the last thing he wanted to be thinking about. He wished he could turn off his heart's feelings. He was sure it was nothing. He didn't celebrate Christmas and he didn't believe in love again. Not anymore. His ship had sailed when his wife passed.

"How does that sound to you, Mrs. Bane?" Evan said to the older woman as she leaned back comfortably in the passenger side seat. "Do you want to visit the Charming Ranch? Or would you like my mother to drop by and stay with you for a while."

Mrs. Bane's eyes lit up; her smile wide. "Yes, dear. I would love that. If it's no trouble. I don't want to pull her away from her family."

"Oh, it's no trouble at all, Ma'am. She would love to visit you."

"Thank you for doing that?" Gwen said to Evan. "I really appreciate it."

"Hey, like I said. It's no trouble at all."

He liked that Gwen treated Mrs. Bane as if she were her own grandmother. Gwen had always had a heart of gold from what he remembered about her in high school. She used to rescue all the little stray pets in the town. He was surprised she didn't go into veterinarian medicine instead of her father's business.

"Well, let's get going. I'll pick up my mother and then we'll head out to Mrs. Bane's house. The flatbed's on its way to your truck."

"Thanks so much again."

Moments later, just as Evan was about to join the ladies in his truck, his cell phone buzzed again as he stood outside his pickup.

He looked at the screen.

His face fell.

It was bad news.

Chapter 5

Well, this charming handsome cowboy knew everything.

A warm glow came over Gwen when she'd watched Evan earlier as he assessed her truck after making sure she and Mrs. Bane were all right.

She snuggled into the seat beside Mrs. Bane. Evan's pickup truck was spacious and very comfy. It had three spacious seats in the back as well as up front.

What would she have done if the Lord hadn't sent this cowboy at the right time? She didn't want to think about it. Her mind came up with all sorts of horrible scenarios of what could have happened.

But he came right in the nick of time. And to that, she would be forever grateful.

Gwen admired that about Evan. Stepping up the plate. Pulling over to help a person out.

Finally, she got a chance to meet up with him again.

She wondered if he even remembered her from high school. Did he? Well, she sure remembered him. But he was off limits then. A Charming brother. And they were off limits to most of the girls in the school. For one thing, he was a senior when she was a junior. Secondly, only the popular girls in school had a chance with him.

Evan was different from all the other guys. She remembered that. He was different from the other Charming brothers, who by the way, all lived up to their name. They were sweet, charismatic cowboys who worked hard and played even harder.

They all left the ranch after high school to pursue college careers as far as she remembered. Evan set up his own ad agency and worked on spreading the message about agriculture. He worked mostly with agricultural clients since he knew so much about the industry, growing up on one of the largest ranches in the district.

A tall, dark and handsome cowboy on a cold and chilly night.

Speaking of which, after she made sure Mrs. Bane was cozy in the passenger seat, she turned her head to look outside to see Evan.

The look on his face concerned her.

Why were his brows furrowed all of a sudden?

"Everything all right?" she asked after he ended his call and got back into the truck.

"I'm afraid not. Looks like the roads are blocked back into town," he said. "A fallen tree."

"Oh, no."

"There's no way we could get Mrs. Bane to the ranch now. We have a lot of rooms at the main house but I don't think we could get there safely," he assessed with a take-charge tone in his voice.

"Are you sure?" Gwen asked.

"Going west is our best bet, right now."

The heavy gusts of winds swept snow all around the truck. The sharp chilly feel of snow pellets had hit her face earlier when she was outside.

She couldn't wait to get home.

Evan excused himself and made another phone call. Probably to let his mother know they wouldn't be back to the ranch.

Gwen remembered he got married a few years back. But then she'd heard his wife died on a mountain climb. How terrible! Her heart went out to him. She heard it was around the holiday time too, if she was not mistaken.

"And?" she asked, curiously.

"Well, the main house is out of reach right now. Tree fell there too."

"We can take Mrs. Bane home, but we have to figure out how to get around the blockage."

"You can stay at my place until the storm blows over," Mrs. Bane said. "I insist. Besides, I don't feel too good being on my own right now. Why don't you two stay for a while."

"That's awfully nice of you, Mrs. Bane. But are you sure?" Evan asked.

"I'm very sure. It would mean a lot to me."

Evan glanced at the screen of his phone.

"We'll be happy to help you out Mrs. Bane and we appreciate the offer of staying for a while. Storm's getting worse right now. The Town just tweeted for everyone to stay indoors."

"Then that settles it," Mrs. Bane said. "Let's stay indoors, at my cabin."

Stay indoors?

Oh, no. Would Mrs. Bane be okay with having visitors in her home tonight? Would she be okay with that?

Could Gwen stay in a small cabin with a cowboy on this stormy night?

Chapter 6

Evan drove off the main road to the back street, hoping to find a way to get safely to Mrs. Bane's cabin on the west side. He'd been there before. The gusts of wind and snow pellets pounded the windshield. His visibility decreased by the moment on this dark snowy night, but he was determined. He prayed to the man upstairs to get them safely to Mrs. Bane's house. Right now, he thought he needed a miracle.

"You ladies all right?" he asked, not taking his eyes off the road blanketed in heavy thick snow. The tires grinded on the crunchy snow.

The ladies nodded and said they were good.

He was careful not to push on the gas too much. He would get there safely.

"You mind if we play some music?" Gwen asked.

"Go right ahead."

"Thanks." Her phone was already charging in his car. She turned on her music on her iPhone. It played some sweet Christmas songs.

He wished he could feel that Christmas spirit, but it was no use. Maybe he should have told her he'd choose the song selection and choose something not so festive.

Mrs. Bane's head rested on the headrest. She looked like she was half asleep.

The scent of Gwen's perfume wafted to his nose. She smelled delicious. What was that fragrance?

His heart reacted to the way her hand brushed his arm as she swiped to get the songs she wanted to play on her phone.

He sucked in a deep breath.

Focus, cowboy.

You shouldn't be feeling anything for Gwen.

"What's your favorite Christmas song?" she asked.

"The First Noel," he said. "What's yours?"

She looked startled.

"What's wrong?"

She grinned. "Nothing. That's my favorite one too. Especially the melody."

"Me too," he said, surprised.

"What's your favorite Christmas memory?" she asked him, probably trying to pass the time as they made their way through the dark snowy night.

"I don't have one."

Now he wasn't being honest, was he?

"Everyone has one."

"I don't. Not anymore."

"But you *do* celebrate it."

"I acknowledge it, of course. But all the parties and get-togethers...Just not for me."

"I'm sorry to hear that. Hope you change your mind later."

"Why?"

"It's such a magical time of the year. Such a special time. There's nothing like the spirit of the season."

"I'm sure. But I just don't feel it. Don't think I ever will."

"What happened to you to make you feel that way?" she probed as if she wanted to fix it.

"I'd rather not get into it, right now."

"I understand." She looked out the window. He could swear he saw the look of hurt in her pretty eyes.

Oh, no. He hoped and prayed he didn't hurt her feelings. That was not his intention. But he didn't want to get into the fact that his wife died over the Christmas holidays and he wasn't even by her side.

He also hoped the drive to Mrs. Bane's cabin would be shorter. He couldn't take all this tension. It wasn't her fault he was grumpy about celebrating the holidays. The lovely lady had a good spirit about her. He just didn't think he deserved to have any of it.

"So," he said to break the silence. "What's *your* favorite holiday memory?" he asked Gwen while Mrs. Bane slept like a baby.

"Family gatherings, church nativity plays. It's always fun. Well, it was when dad was around."

"I'm really sorry for your loss. Cam was a good man."

"Thank you. He passed around the holidays last year."

"Man, I'm really sorry about that."

"It's okay." She waited for him to say something else. He could sense that. But he wasn't' ready to talk about his late wife.

He's sure Gwen must have heard about the accident on the mountain. The whole town heard. But then again, maybe Gwen was out of town at the time.

Later, on the drive, Mrs. Bane woke up. She and Gwen started singing Christmas carols as they drove through the snow-covered roads towards Mrs. Bane's cabin.

Evan wanted to feel the spirit. But he just couldn't. Guilt prevented him from doing that. Still, the lovely lips and breathtaking smile on Gwen's face and they she lit up as they sang, made him feel something inside. But he had to push those feelings away.

Finally, they made it to the Bane's cabin. The driveway was filled with about a foot of snow.

Evan got out of the truck and grabbed his shovel in the back. Then he began shovelling.

"Oh, dear. The snow is so high," Mrs. Bane said as Gwen helped her out of the truck. "I didn't get to put salt on the driveway."

"No problem, Mrs. Bane," Evan said.

"Please be careful."

"I will, Ma'am." Evan shovelled a pathway first to get Mrs. Bane safely inside. After Gwen helped Mrs. Bane up the walkway to her home, Evan continued to shovel the driveway.

"Please be careful," Mrs. Bane said again, this time from the top of her steps as she stood by the door to go inside. "It's slippery."

"I will..." Evan said again, this time, his boots went up as he slipped on the driveway.

Evan shook his head and grinned, trying to ignore the sharp pain in his side.

Great. This was really great.

"Oh, no. Are you all right?" Gwen called out from the top of the steps after Mrs. Bane was safely inside.

"Just thought I'd look up at the stars while laying on my back," he teased.

Gwen burst out laughing and came down to help him.

He propped himself to sit up.

He just wanted to sit there for a second. As he sat up on the driveway, he heard steps beside him crunching in the snow. It was Gwen standing there with her hand help out for him to get up.

She certainly was quite a girl.

He could get up on his own, of course. But he held out his gloved hand. And she took his. He stood up. There was a nice feeling holding her hand. He tried to tell her to stand still, but it was too late, she moved one boot and she went down too.

"Are you all right?" he asked, trying to catch her fall—but they both landed down on the slippery ground.

She burst out laughing as the wind blew snow around them.

"Well, isn't this something," she said.

He actually liked the feeling of holding her in his arms. There was something that felt comfortable about Gwen. A strange yet delightful feeling swirled around him. What was that feeling? He wasn't supposed to be feeling anything this year. Nothing at all.

Just then, after they'd both propped themselves back up on the driveway, holding each other, she bent down to scoop up a ball of fresh snow in her hands.

Oh, no.

She hurled a snowball towards him.

He scooped up snow as well. "So this is how it's going down, huh?" he asked, jokingly.

She placed her hands on her hips. Then she bent down on grabbed some more snow.

"Thanks for the fall," she joked, and hurled snow at him.

He did the same and scooped up some snow and gently tossed it in her direction.

"That's all you've got?" she laughed, hands on her hips.

"Didn't want to hurt you. You know, you being a girl and all."

"Oh, really now? You think I'm fragile, do you?" She grabbed an even larger ball of snow.

Before long they were laughing and engaged in a lovely snowball fight.

He couldn't' remember the last time he had so much fun.

A light energy came over him.

It was as if his late wife was telling him, it's okay. It's okay to move forward and get on with your life. It was as if she was up in heaven looking down on him, giving him her approval. Letting him know she was all right where she was.

Lightness came over his heart. Would this last?

***

"What's this?" Evan said later inside the cabin. Earlier, they'd finished up their snowball fight and cleaned up the driveway so the snow wouldn't accumulate too much by the morning.

He was stunned to see the place so beautifully decorated. He didn't want to be reminded of Christmas again. He already did his part to decorate the ranch. But this little cozy cottage was a winter wonderland.

"You like?" Gwen said, cheerfully, taking off her jacket and hat and scarf and gloves and placing them by the side on the coat rack. "I helped Mrs. Bane decorate her cottage for the holiday the other day."

"You did all this?" He was surprised. He didn't think the cute tow truck driver had time to pretty up someone's cottage. Christmas and the winter season were the busiest times of the year in Mistletoe for the tow truck industry.

"Sure did." She paused for a moment as if studying his face. "You're not too happy." It sounded more like a statement than a question.

"Oh, no. I just...It's okay."

She wanted to say something else, but...she didn't.

"I had fun out there tonight," Gwen said. "Never thought I'd have a belly laugh like that in a long while. Not after, well...my dad passed...."

"Of course. It must be hard."

"Some days are better than others. He was always into the Christmas spirit and his laugh was infectious," she said.

Just like yours, he wanted to say.

Just then Mrs. Bane came out with a tray of hot chocolate and freshly baked biscuits.

"When did you make these? I thought you were asleep," Gwen said, surprised.

"Oh, I wanted to make you both something for being so kind staying here with me until the storm settles down to make sure I'm all right. And you must be cold after shovelling my driveway."

"It was no problem, Mrs. Bane," Evan said.

"Yes, it was no problem at all."

"Here you go," she said, placing the tray down.

"Thank you so much," they both said in unison.

Mrs. Bane had a wide grin on her lips. And Evan thought he saw a wink in her left eye. Or was that his imagination?

"Aren't you having any?" Evan asked as he helped Mrs. Bane take the mugs off the tray and onto the table.

"Oh, I'm fine," she said. "You two enjoy your hot chocolate and biscuits. Let me know if you need anything else. I'm going upstairs to rest a little."

"Of course, no trouble."

The trays had lovely gingerbread cookies laid out beautifully just as his mother used to make. The hot chocolates had a candy cane inside each cup, topped with fresh whipped cream.

"That's awfully kind of you, Mrs. Bane."

"Think nothing of it. See you both later." She made her way upstairs as Evan and Gwen sat down in the living room.

Oh, boy.

If he didn't know any better, he'd swear Mrs. Bane had something up her sleeve. He was willing to bet she was about to call his mother.

Now, what was he going to talk to Gwen about?

Chapter 7

There was an awkward silence between Evan and Gwen for a moment after Mrs. Bane left them alone in the living room.

"Lovely tree," he commented.

"Thanks. It's not finished. Would you like to help me finish decorating it?"

She walked over to the corner to pick up a large box of ornaments.

"Here, let me help you with that," he said.

He placed his cup down on the table and walked over to where she was. He scooped up the heavy box and their hands brushed for the first time without gloves. He felt a tingle inside.

"Sorry," she said.

"For what?"

"Oh, nothing."

A moment lingered between them. Evan couldn't help but notice she had the prettiest blue eyes he'd ever seen. Her eyes were blue as a cloudless sky on a warm summer day.

"These are nice," he said, after he placed the box down beside the tree and opened it.

"I got some of the items from the market. And some of them are from Mrs. Bane's old house in the attic. They mean a lot to her."

"It's very nice of you to help her out."

"It's nothing. Mrs. Bane was also a friend of my dad. And I miss my Grandma who passed away when I was much younger. Mrs. Bane became another grandma to me in a way."

His heart melted at her warmth and her sentimentality.

"You're good with taking care of people," he commented, wanting to know more about the girl he hardly knew in high school. The girl who always mesmerized him from afar.

"Thanks. I took care of my dad last year when..."

"I know it must be difficult," he said, his voice soft and low.

"Yes, it was."

Her eyes misted.

He wanted to hug her, to comfort her.

But she wiped her eyes and started to place another ornament on the tree.

"I was out of town on business when it happened. When he got the call from the doctor," she said, fixing up one of the branches on the tree. "So, I left my job and came back here to take care of him. To be with him."

"That was very nice of you."

He'd never met a girl like that who'd sacrifice so much. Just give up everything to help a loved one. A parent.

Then again, if he were in her shoes, he'd probably do the same thing.

"My father gave so much to the family. He always took care of us. It was the least I could do. I didn't want him to be all alone." Her tone sounded stronger.

She tried to put up a brave front but he could tell in her eyes, she was still hurting. He knew a thing or two about the pain of losing someone close to you.

She looked stunning against the backdrop of the beautifully lit Christmas tree with the lovely flickering lights, like a million tiny lightbulbs.

"So that's why you took over the tow-truck business?"

"I had no choice. Dad made it clear when he knew he didn't have much time that he didn't want the Altons to buy him out."

"The Altons?" Evan was stunned. "What do they have to do with this?"

His family knew the Altons very well. They were considered loan sharks and they sometimes went under another name as alternate lenders. They were more like dangerous lenders.

They weren't the nicest people in town. In fact, he'd had some run-ins with them before when they tried to blackmail his now late father. They gave his old man a lot of stress. He had to have a few words with them about that. And it wasn't pretty. They backed off eventually. But he hoped no one else he knew would get involved with them, if he could help it.

"My dad borrowed money from them when things were slow during the recession."

"I see." Evan clenched his jaw.

"He regretted every moment he owed them," she continued. "The interest rates were out of this world. He ended up owing more than double the amount he borrowed. I wished I'd known then. But my dad was so proud that he didn't tell anyone else about it at the time."

"So what happened to the loan?"

"He couldn't pay it off. And I had helped him with his medical bills…"

Evan's heart squeezed in his chest. He really felt her pain. He wanted to comfort her, to hold her, to let her know she'd done good by her dad and that he wanted to help her the rest of the way. He listened attentively, admiring her, wanting to be there for her.

He didn't know why this feeling came over him. Ever since his wife passed, he wanted nothing to do with anyone, especially women. He just wanted to close himself off from the world. But Gwen was a different story. All of a sudden, he wanted to be in her world.

Why was he feeling this way?

He couldn't save his now late wife, but maybe he could save Gwen—in a different way.

He told everyone he no longer felt the Christmas spirit, but he was beginning to rethink that.

"So," she continued "I gave up my condo and my job and contacted my dad's loyal customers and let them know I would be taking over. They were relieved to hear that. No one wanted to deal with the Altons."

"I don't blame them," he added.

He wanted to know if there was someone in her life who was there for her at the time.

But she answered his question as if she could hear this thoughts.

"My ex had left me at the time."

"I'm sorry to hear that."

"No, I'm not. It was for the best. He couldn't handle a woman doing a so-called man's job."

"That's too bad for him. His loss. You don't need a guy like that."

"Thank you. He also left with some of my savings. But that's okay. You live and you learn."

"What did he do?" Fury surged through Evan. He disliked when a man took advantage of a woman's kindness. It robbed him the wrong way.

"Some scheme, he wanted me to invest in. Like I said, I'm not bothered by it now. Things can turnaround anytime. Just got to have a little faith and put in a little work."

"True." He agreed.

She grinned. "Unfortunately, we didn't have many funds to get a new fleet of tow trucks and as you found out, the one I'm driving is pretty old, in bad shape."

"Listen, don't worry about that. I've got you covered."

"You? Oh, no." She shook her head. "I can't do that. You've done enough already."

"Seriously, it's no big deal. My friend's working on your truck now. Please don't worry about the charge. Besides, I owe your old man one." A smile touched his lips. "He'd helped me out on quite a few tows during the day. Especially when I got my first car." He chuckled.

She grinned. "Your first car? That was you?" She placed her hands on her hips. "Did you happen to drive an old Sunfire back in the day?"

He smiled. "That thing got me from point A to B."

"And C," she added. "Dad told me about a young guy with a Sunfire that had its days in the sun."

"Yeah. In the sun and in the ditch. A long time ago."

They both grinned and looked into each other's eyes. They locked gaze for a moment and he felt his heart beat faster.

"So...what about you?" she said, as she placed more ornaments on the Christmas tree.

He noticed a hint of rouge on her lovely cheeks.

"You don't work on the ranch, do you?" she said. "I haven't seen you around."

"I do. Sometimes I help out. I grew up on the ranch. But right now, I have my own business, spreading awareness about agriculture and helping other businesses."

"Advertising. That's right. I heard that one of the Charmings had an ad agency. That's sweet. Must be a lot of fun putting those campaigns together."

He paused for a moment. Was it fun? In the beginning it was. But now it was a place to bury his head, not wanting to deal with the reality that his beloved wife was gone.

And speaking of which, he was supposed to be in the office working on a campaign for the new year for one of his clients. He didn't like the fact that he was going to be spending the holidays in his office building instead of on the ranch with his family.

Guilt swept over him. His mother wanted him to be there for the Christmas Barn Hall Dance and he'd told her he'd be working. He didn't want to show up alone. He didn't want to enjoy the celebration.

"It was a lot of fun, until..." His voice broke off.

"Are you all right?" Her voice was soft.

"My wife passed last year, around the holidays."

"Oh, Evan. I'm so sorry for your loss." Her genuine expression of sorrow gave him some comfort.

"I know what it's like to lose a loved one over the holidays," she added. "I know it can't be easy. I can't imagine a spouse."

"Thank you," he said softly.

"Your wife is with the Lord know. Just my like Dad."

Just then, he felt comfort wrap around him.

"Yes, they are," he agreed.

He knew he should have felt some comfort before. But he refused to feel anything but anger at the time, but as the year passed, he'd gotten used to the fact that his beloved wife was not coming back. But she was up in heaven now. He had to find some way to move forward. But it was hard. Guilt was a hard pill to swallow.

"Are you going to be all right?" she asked.

"I felt like it was my fault she's not here now."

Her face looked alarmed. "Why do you say that?"

"She was on a mountain climbing trip. And I was busy working at the office on a campaign and I didn't want to go with her..."

"Oh, no. I'm so sorry to hear that. But Evan, you have to know it's not your fault."

"Isn't it?" he said, but instantly felt regret that he snapped at his new friend.

"No. It isn't. Do you know why?"

"Why?"

"Because you cannot predict the future. None of us can. You had no idea what was going to happen. I heard about that accident on the mountain side. It was terrible. I don't know what I could say to let you know that you couldn't have known."

"You're right, but I feel as if..."

"As if what?" she asked gently. And he instantly felt soothed by her lovely warm tone as warm as honey.

"Maybe I don't want to feel happy."

"I think your late wife would have wanted you to be okay."

It was as if his wife was around them, her spirit anyway. And it was as if she was telling Evan it's all right.

"She loved mountain climbing right? Her name was Rhonda, right?"

"Yes."

She sucked in a deep breath. "I can't believe it's the same lady. Do you know something?"

"What is it?"

"I actually towed her car once.'

"That was you? I was out of town on business once, when she told me her car broke down, but the tow person was kind and gave her a ride to finish her shopping."

He felt warm that this tow truck lady was so kind and caring.

"Yes, I'd taken over my dad's business while he was sick the last two years of his life. And I got a chance to meet your late wife. She was lovely. And do you know what she told me."

"What did she tell you?"

"That life's an adventure. She loved living it."

His heart exploded with emotion in his chest.

It was as if Rhonda was speaking through Gwen.

"Yes, she always said that," he commented with a smile.

"That means you should have comfort in knowing that she lived her life the way she wanted to. And she left here doing something she lived for..."

She was right.

It was as if the Lord brought Gwen into his life right now for a reason.

"You know something, I've never thought about it that way after that...incident."

She touched his arm and he felt a wave of emotion. A good emotion. The spirit of the season. It was as if his guilt had washed away. But he wanted to do more for Gwen now. She had no idea what she'd just done for him.

"I wish I could do something special for you."

"I think you already have."

Here was this beautiful tow truck driver with a heart of gold and warmth and love and insight. He wanted to see her again.

But maybe he should ask her to the barn dance. No, it's probably a bad idea to even think of asking Gwen. Or maybe it wasn't.

"Gwen, would you like to come with me to the Christmas Barn Hall Dance?"

She took a deep breath. "I'm sorry. I...I can't."

She looked very sorry she had to turn him down.

His heart sank.

"No problem," he said casually, trying to brush off it. "Just thought I'd ask."

Was he ever going to see Gwen again?

Chapter 8

After the snowstorm settled and Mrs. Bane was comfortable, Evan checked around the house with Gwen to make sure everything was safe.

"Okay, looks like we're done here." He and Gwen told Mrs. Bane goodbye and to call them if she needed anything.

Gwen appreciated this cowboy's take charge and caring demeanor. She also appreciated him spending extra time with her and Mrs. Bane. And for taking care of her tow truck.

"You are really amazing, you know that cowboy," Gwen said to Evan after they sat in his truck.

"I am?"

"Yes, you did a lot tonight helping us out and then staying with us long after the storm settled down."

"Hey, it was nothing. Anytime."

"Do you mean that?"

"I wouldn't say it if I didn't," the cowboy grinned and she saw the lovely smile on his lips.

Those lips of his.

She was embarrassed to admit, she wondered what they would feel like on hers.

Okay, calm down now Gwen. He's probably unavailable. Emotionally.

He was a widower, after all. And who could blame him for taking his time?

He had, however, invited her to the barn dance.

She told him she couldn't go. Why did she say that?

Was she afraid of dating again?

She wished she could go. She really liked him. A lot. But she had work to do. Christmas holidays was her company's busiest season. There was no way she could slack off now.

"So, where to?" he asked.

She gave him her address.

"Are you sure, you'll be all right tonight?" Evan asked Gwen later when they arrived at her home. The home she grew up in. The home her father spent his last days.

She noticed Evan's eyebrows furrowed with concern.

Was he worried about her? That was so sweet of him.

She sighed deeply.

"Yes. I will be fine," she said.

Though deep down, she wished they could chat over a cup of coffee. Just like they'd done over at Mrs. Bane's house. But it was getting late. And she had to be up early to check on what's happening with her tow truck. And he probably had work to do to. He'd told her that he had been on his way to his office when he saw her stranded on the roadside with Mrs. Bane.

Was he going to go back to the office now?

"That's the house I grew up in," she said. "I'll make sure everything's locked up."

"I can come and look around the house first, if you like?"

"That's so sweet of you. I'm fine. Really."

"Okay, but I'll be waiting out here until you give me the signal you're good. Deal?"

She grinned. Was he charming or what?

"Deal?"

Gwen walked into the home and turned on her lights, while Evan waited outside his truck. Ready to come in if she needed him.

When she turned on the lights. She screamed.

Chapter 9

"What the...?"

The scream coming from Gwen's house caused Evan to rush from his truck towards the direction of the sound.

"Are you all right?" he asked once he got inside the front door and held her.

She then shook her head and grinned. "I'm sorry, Evan."

Evan's eyes followed her gaze.

A man sat in the corner of the living room. He looked as if he hadn't shaved in years.

"Who are you?" Evan asked, firmly. "What are you doing here?"

"I'm just here to see my little sister," he said, his hands up in the air as if he was surrendering.

"Is this man your brother?" Evan asked, surprised. He didn't realize old man Cam had more than one child. He thought he didn't have a son.

"Yes, he's my half-brother. My mother had a child before she met my father. My brother and I just got to know each other a few years back."

He surveyed Gwen's face to make sure she was okay.

"I'm really sorry to scare you sis, really." The man looked apologetic.

The man seemed harmless enough and very sorry. And very frail.

"No worries. What are you doing in town?" She then asked. "I'm glad to see you but with you breaking into my home and surprising me like this..."

"Man, I'm so sorry. I wanted to surprise you, not scare you. And I didn't break in. The back door was open."

She gave him a really-now look.

"Is that true?" Evan asked, wanting nothing more than to protect her.

"Yes. Sometimes I leave the back door open..."

Evan politely interjected. "I wish you wouldn't do that. It's not safe. It's a small town and everybody knows everybody, but you never know...There are a lot of visitors coming in and out of town every day."

"True," she agreed. "Listen, I'm fine. You can leave. I know you must have a lot of work to do."

"Just as long as you're fine."

"I am."

Just then the image of his wife, flashed in his mind.

Gwen smiled with appreciation. "That's very sweet of you to offer, but we're good."

***

"You like him, don't you?" her brother Rex said later.

"He's a nice cowboy." Gwen smiled.

"And you like him."

"I like him as a friend."

"Oh, come on. I can tell the way you two look at each other. You both look like you're connected."

"Connected?" she asked, making a fresh pot of tea.

"Yes."

"Okay, don't change the subject. What are you doing here? And why did you break into my house?"

"Babs left me."

"Oh, no. I'm so sorry to hear that."

"Well, actually, she kicked me out. I need a place to stay."

"You can stay here as long as you like."

"Thanks, sis."

She poured their cups with steaming hot tea. Perfect for a wintery night like tonight. It was a good thing Evan was around at the time though. What if it *had* been an intruder. She shuddered to think about that.

"What's on your mind, sis? You're in a daze."

"I am not."

"When are you two going out?"

"We're not."

"And why not? He seems like a nice guy. A lot nicer than that rat you dated a few years back when I first met you."

"Yes, Evan is so much nicer. But..."

"But what?"

"I'm not ready to date again. I've got to focus on keeping Dad's business afloat."

"That doesn't mean you can't share your journey with someone. I just felt something there between you two. I like the way he was going to throw me out on my behind if I was an intruder."

Gwen smiled.

"I mean, I wouldn't have liked it, but I like that he's looking out for my little sis."

She did appreciate Evan's protectiveness and his support. But she didn't want to get too close to another man again. Her heart was still healing after her ex. She really should focus on her business.

But what if she missed her chance at happiness again?

Was it too late?

Evan would probably meet someone else at his family's Christmas barn dance. It was too late. She'd already told the cowboy, no.

She was never going to see him again.

Chapter 10

"So, you decided to show up this year?" Evan's brother Cameron said to him the following week at the Charming Ranch Annual Christmas Barn Hall Dance.

He missed last year, after Rhonda passed. And he'd vowed to never attend again. But here he was.

Holiday music was sounding through the speakers and guests were filing in. At least he made it, but he didn't feel as if he were there spiritually. Just physically. Maybe it would take some time to get into the groove of things again.

His thoughts were also on Gwen. Maybe she was busy with the tow service. She had business to tend to, after all.

Last week, he'd made sure that she got her truck in pristine condition. She was very thankful. But then he hadn't seen her since. He'd been back at the office working on his latest client's proposal for a new year campaign. And all that time, his mind was on Gwen.

"What's wrong?" Cameron asked.

Evan couldn't help the feeling of sadness that washed over him. The truth was, he missed Gwen's company. That day in the snow and while they were helping Mrs. Bane meant a lot to him. He hadn't smiled or connected with anyone in a long while and he knew now that he'd been missing something. He had so much fun that day—and he could tell that she did too. He'd thought the Lord brought two lost souls who'd lost loved ones together for a reason. But maybe it wasn't meant to last. Just a flash in the pan.

If he were being honest with himself, he would love to see Gwen again.

He would love to have that kiss under the mistletoe.

The magic of the Charming Ranch mistletoe kiss was that those who kissed under it would be blessed with a long and happy relationship.

Yes, it was true that ancient cultures revered the mistletoe for its healing properties and it was always a sign of good luck to those who kissed under it.

Last week, Evan had offered to have someone fill in for Gwen so she could have some fun and come to the barn hall dance.

Everyone in the community who attended always had a blast. She'd told him she would love to go to the dance but was afraid of business slipping during a busy time, so she had to decline his offer.

No problem, he thought. But there was a problem. He was missing her like crazy. And he wanted her to relax at least one day during the holiday season. She seemed to be working overtime everyday catching up on work. She was a trooper. And he admired that about her.

"Darling son, I'm so glad you came," his mother said.

"I'm happy to be here."

"You never know, you might find that special someone to kiss under the mistletoe this year."

His mother always tried to play matchmaker for her sons. Just then he saw Mrs. Bane.

"Well, Mrs. Bane, how are you doing?" he asked.

"Never better. Thank you again for rescuing me last week."

"Oh, it was my pleasure."

"Oh, no. It was *my* pleasure. I love bringing people together." She winked.

He had no idea why Mrs. Bane winked just now. Only that she was a sly little matchmaker.

The party was a success. But it was getting late. And Evan wanted to return to his office.

When Evan turned around to leave. His jaw fell open.

There she was. A stunning beauty.

Wow!

Gwen strolled through the door like a princess. Her lovely mane of hair swept up in a gracious style. Her face pretty as a princess. Her gown hugged her body, showing off her lovely curves.

He was stunned into silence.

"You came," he said, walking closer to her.

"I thought about what you said. And well, I took up your offer. Your friend is covering for me. I can't thank you enough."

"Hey, it's my pleasure. I'm glad you're here."

"Me too,."

"You look *beautiful*. Amazing," he complimented.

"Thank you. So do you," she gushed. "I mean, handsome. You look handsome in your suit."

He thanked her for her compliment.

Moments later, Evan saw Mrs. Bane and his mother eyeing him and Gwen lovingly as the couple danced.

He couldn't help but grin.

He loved the scent of Gwen's perfume. Her smooth skin touched his as they slow danced.

He just realized as Mrs. Bane and his mother talked in a corner looking over at them, grinning, that Mrs. Bane probably wanted them to talk that night she asked both of them to stay in her living room over a cup of hot chocolate.

A warm smile curved his lips.

"This is wonderful," Gwen said. "I hope we can see each other after this."

"I would like that," he said.

She looked up and smiled.

"Isn't that the famous mistletoe?"

He too looked up. "It sure is."

"How about it, cowboy?"

She leaned up to him and he leaned down.

He could not believe this was happening.

He brushed his lips over hers and they shared the most memorable kiss ever. He tingled inside after their kiss.

It was magical.

Special.

A true blessing to be given a second chance.

Evan believed in the magic of Christmas again. The Christmas spirit came over him once more. He looked forward to spending more time with Gwen. He knew one thing for sure, he was never going to stop counting his blessings.

COWBOY FOR CHRISTMAS

Rescued by the Cowboy at Christmas - Book 3
By J. A. Somers

COWBOY FOR CHRISTMAS

Cameron Charming is going to put Christmas on hold this year and focus on his work instead. He'd lost his family during the holidays a while back. His plans to remain grumpy over the Christmas season are thwarted when he meets a charming red-headed beauty with a fiery personality.

Seriously? Cat cannot believe her luck. She's stuck outside in the small town of Mistletoe over the holidays. The blogger-turned-author has a tight deadline to meet but she can't get into her cozy cabin to finish her manuscript. And to top it off, a terrible storm is brewing. Then...a handsome cowboy shows up.

Can two people, determined to remain single, get caught up in the spirit of the Christmas season?

Chapter 1

Oh no! This can't be happening!

Catherine "Cat" Smith could not believe her luck. She blew out a puff of air in the dark wintery night sky as she sighed heavily. The key was stuck in the lock of her cabin's front door.

Her teeth clattered as she fought to keep warm.

What was she going to do now?

She could not believe this was happening. She had just gotten back to her hometown of Mistletoe after signing her first book deal. Her publisher had given her an advance and she decided the perfect writing spot to finish her manuscript would be in this rented cabin for a month—away from distraction. She lived in New York with her roommates and there was no way she could get the book done in time for the deadline if she stayed there with all the noise.

The money from the advance was generous and it not only paid for the cabin for the month of December but it was enough to cover the fees for her grandfather's care at the retirement home in New York for the next twelve months. She'd been taking care of him with the money she'd been making from her blog ever since his stroke and since her grandmother had passed.

When her folks passed when she was in her teens, her grandfather had raised her. She would do anything for him. She was glad she was in a position to be there for him and to help him too. In fact, he always encouraged her to follow her dream of writing for a living.

Luckily, being a content creator, she could work from anywhere as long as she had a laptop computer, Wi-Fi connection and electricity.

Right now, she could use some Wi-Fi *and* some electricity to keep her warm.

She tried the lock again. The key still wouldn't work. Her agent had arranged for her cabin retreat and accommodation in Mistletoe. Did he send her the wrong key?

She had to turn in the final draft of her book by Christmas. Her book was due to be released in the new year by February. The publishers were aiming for a Valentine's Day release.

It was ironic that it was a Valentine's Day release since Cat no longer believed in love.

After her ex-fiancé broke off with her after he got what he wanted out of her when she helped him with his college studies, she decided to focus on her own life and help others in the same boat—that's when she created her Singles blog.

How could she have not seen that her ex had been using her? She had pushed her dreams aside while helping him with his—only for him to turn around and dump her for some dancer.

Well, so much for putting her heart on the line. Never again. She was going to focus on her career and taking care of Grandpa. She had no room in her life for anyone else right now.

It was already four weeks till Christmas but that was the best time to be locked away in a cabin, away from holiday carollers and everybody else making a fuss about Christmas. Her grandfather and she stopped celebrating the holiday years ago when her grandmother passed.

She didn't know if she could ever feel the Christmas spirit again since her ex broke off with her over the holidays.

And right now, she knew that Christmas could be hard on the lonely. That's why she decided to distance herself from everyone else right now and focus on her material.

The truth was, she'd hoped to be married by thirty-five. It was her dream to be as happy as her parents were before they went to be with the Lord. But to make herself feel better and protect her heart from any more heartbreak she decided maybe it wasn't for her. She wished she had some sort of sign though. Maybe she should just forget about relationships and help others with theirs. No matter how much she told herself it didn't matter if she never found that special one, there was something inside her, a loneliness that swept over her.

Speaking of sweeping over her. The snow came down heavy like a bale of hay. The chill prickled her skin on her exposed cheeks. She rubbed herself as she shivered outside.

She reached into her bag to pull out her cell phone.

It was dead.

Dead.

Just as she would be soon if she didn't get inside soon, away from the plummeting temperatures.

Her agent was supposed to have everything arranged now including a key that worked. And if she had any power left on her cell phone, she'd call him now and give him a piece of her mind.

She prayed to the Lord to keep her safe out there. She glanced around and it was pitch dark. The streetlights were dimly lit and didn't provide too much light.

Why, oh, why did she tell the Uber driver to leave once she arrived at her destination? She should have told him to wait to see if she could get inside first.

Cat rubbed her arms as she shivered to keep warm. Ice pellets touched her exposed skin on her face.

Right now she wished she was inside her cabin, nice and warm. On nights like this, she was reminded of the times when she *did* celebrate the holidays with her grandparents. She would come in from the bitter winter cold and into the home. Her grandmother would bake the most delicious gingerbread cookies and Cat would love to eat them as soon as they came out of the oven. The aroma of the gingerbread always comforted her. The cookies were always fresh, crispy and warm. Just as warm as she wished she was right now.

Why did that memory sweep into her mind all of a sudden?

She wanted to be comforted. Remembering happier, simpler times.

She then started to walk, her boots crunching on the snow, as she tried to figure out if the back door was open. She didn't think so, of course, but she had no choice but to try.

"Okay, there has to be a way to get inside."

Maybe she should see if there was an opened window she could climb into. She'd already paid for the whole month to rent this cabin. And it wasn't cheap, either.

Just then, she heard a sound coming from the back of the cabin. Was someone hiding back there?

She froze.

Chapter 2

Cameron Charming made his way up the steps to the Children's Center at the Mistletoe Hospital carrying a large red sack full of Christmas presents.

The security guard at the front desk nodded and let him through since he'd been there earlier. He was a regular there.

He'd been volunteering his time there ever since he lost his wife and stepdaughter many years ago in a freak car accident over the holidays. He thought he'd never want to celebrate the holidays again but he'd learned that helping others was a great way to give back and to help in the healing process.

Volunteering his time gave him a chance to reach out to others during their difficult time and to give a helping hand to families in the community.

He walked into the main activity room where the kids were gathered around for storytelling. The place was decorated in twinkling red and green Christmas lights and the fireplace in the corner had lovely red velvet stockings that hung around it. The garland around the electric fireplace reminded him of the one at the main house on the ranch. It gave one a lovely feeling of warmth and joy around the holidays.

In no time, a few of the kids rushed over to him and greeted him.

Seeing their bright smiles when he brought presents for them warmed his heart.

The kids unwrapped their presents with excitement.

Lia, the senior coordinator came by and thanked him again.

"How are you keeping up?" Lia asked him later after he'd finished spending an hour there. She walked with him as he made his way out to the main foyer of the building.

"Good," he said.

"I know it can't be easy for you," she said. "But we really appreciate you coming here every year."

"I'm just glad I could make it," he added.

She smiled.

"Are you coming to the Annual Christmas Barn Hall Dance?" he asked her once they got to the main doors.

"Wouldn't miss it for the world."

Lia was about the same age as his mother. A very nice lady. And like his mother, Lia had tried to play matchmaker for him, telling him it would be nice to move forward. He'd thanked her but told her he was not going to think about relationships for now. Even though it had been four years now to the day. He just wasn't interested in anyone.

"I hope to see you under the magical mistletoe this year," Lia said with a warm smile.

"I don't think that's going to happen, Miss Lia. I think I've passed those days."

"You never know. It's been magical for your brothers." She arched a brow with a grin.

He was happy his brothers had finally found love under the mistletoe during the family's annual Christmas dance. That famous mistletoe always bestowed good luck to those who kissed under it. But this cowboy was sure it wasn't going to happen for him anytime soon. He just didn't feel right moving on. He wanted to hold a candle to his late wife and stepdaughter forever. That's how he felt in his heart right now.

He knew deep down that's not the way the Lord wanted him to live his life. But he had so many issues to work through and he knew it was going to take time. A lot of time.

He placed his cowboy hat back on his head and made his way out the door of the north wing of the hospital, out into the cold winter night.

"Thanks again for coming, Cameron. It's always nice to see you."

"Likewise, Lia."

"And think about what I said. You never know who you'll meet at the dance." She winked.

Oh, boy.

He grinned and shook his head.

That clearly meant Lia had someone in mind for him. Once again.

He didn't want to hurt anyone's feelings though.

But maybe soon they'd see that he was serious when he said he wasn't going to be in another relationship again. Not after losing his family. He just didn't feel right moving on or being happy when they couldn't be here.

Would he ever get over that feeling?

Chapter 3

Cat's heart stopped beating. Her breath halted.

"Who's there?" she called out into the cold dark night as snow blew around her. Too bad the lights in her cabin were off. Of course there was no light inside. She wasn't inside to turn them on. No one was inside. But someone *was* outside her house.

Who was it? A burglar?

She hoped not. They wouldn't find anything inside to take.

But right now she was on deadline with her book and had to turn in her first draft, as per her contract.

"Who's there?" Her voice sounded bolder and stronger. She wasn't afraid. Well, actually, she was, but she wasn't going to let anyone know.

Her handbag was heavy. In fact, her friends always teased her that she could knock someone out with her handbag if she wasn't careful. She held it up to her chest, getting ready to swing it at the intruder.

But it was too late. Something came out at her and she screamed.

It moved quickly and rushed past her.

Oh, thank goodness.

It was a racoon, not an intruder.

Wait a minute. Why was she thankful it was a racoon? It wasn't like he had a key with him or anything to help her get inside her warm cabin.

Well, she assumed it would be warmer inside than outside.

Pushing herself against the heavy winds blowing in her direction, she made her way up the steps leading to the side of the cabin.

Her skin prickled with ice as snow pellets continued to blow around her as if they were attacking her personally.

When she finally climbed toward the back of the cabin, her jaw fell wide open.

Chapter 4

Cameron decided to avoid the town's heavy traffic. He wanted to have a long quiet drive home back to Charming Ranch.

He needed time to think.

He started down on West Street when for some strange reason, he turned down East Street. Why did he do that?

He thought nothing of it at the time. He wanted a long quiet drive so he was going to get one. East Street was more country and had a few cabins spattered about. It was where a lot of recluse people lived. Those who wanted to be closer to nothing but nature and far away from noise in the heaviest part of town.

He couldn't blame them one bit.

Just then a sound came from his truck.

It was his cell phone ringing through the speakers. He had it set up so he didn't have to reach to answer it while driving. His late wife had been the one to insist he have it done. She saved his life.

But he didn't save hers. Or their daughter.

You weren't there, man. You couldn't have saved them. You weren't there.

Well, those words echoing in his mind sure didn't make him feel any better. He should've been there. He should have been there to rescue them, to comfort them, to let them know he was there and everything was going to be all right.

But he didn't.

He couldn't.

And he'd have to live with that guilt for the rest of his life.

The Lord had blessed him with a wonderful family. And look what happened. He was away on business at the time.

He was a broken cowboy.

Too broken to ever love again. He just didn't feel he could ever move forward.

He sighed deeply.

"Hey, what's up?"

"What? No Merry Christmas?" That was the ever-sarcastic voice of his brother Brad.

"No Merry Christmas. You've got that right," Cameron responded.

"Come on, man," his other brother Carter said. They obviously had him on speaker phone.

He was happy for Carter who, after breaking up with his fiancée some Christmases ago, reunited with her and got married. She'd come back one Christmas and explained why she had to break off with him and now they were happily married with a baby on the way.

If there was ever someone who deserved it, it was Carter. And all his brothers, as a matter of fact. They'd all had their share of heartbreak and now they were happily married.

He'd had his chance. He often wondered if that was the only chance at being happily married he'd get.

Did everyone just get one shot at it?

Well, maybe just some people, of which he was probably one of them.

He couldn't save his family. Now there was nothing inside him. Maybe that was his last chance and he blew it.

"Sorry Carter and Brad. I'm just not feeling it right now."

"But Lia said it went well at the Children's Hospital. She said you were in the festive mood. Didn't it go well?"

"It did. You should've seen the look on the kids' faces. It was a pure blessing."

"So what happened? Why are you so down then?" Carter asked.

"Because after I leave, the feeling leaves. It's happened that way ever since..."

He paused and said nothing for a moment. The only sound that could be heard was the sound of the four wheels grinding on the road on this snowy winter night. He wished his family was with him now.

"Man, I'm really sorry. I know it can't be easy. Especially at this time of the year," Carter offered.

"It will get better, man," his brother Brad also added over the speaker phone.

"Will it?"

"It sure will. Give it time. You've been through a lot. Nothing can replace your family, but with time, you can move forward you know. Look at Evan."

"True. But he found someone."

"And he forgave himself for not being there when...well, you know."

"I know." Cameron's voice was soft and low. He didn't need them to continue on. He knew how heartbroken and crushed his brother Evan had been when his wife died while on a mountain climb. A climb that they were supposed to do together with their group. But it never happened. And like Cameron, he wasn't there for his loved one, when they were in grave danger.

He appreciated what his brothers were trying to do for him, by encouraging him. He really did. But this was something that was going to take time with him. He knew that. He could not skip any of the steps of grieving. But the trouble was, he felt stuck on one step. Denial.

"Well, you know I've got to take this long drive."

"Don't tell me you're out on the country road again."

"Just want to clear my mind. Going back to my cabin's just going to give me too much time to think."

"Maybe thinking is good. Sometimes," Brad offered.

"I don't know about now," Carter interjected. "Have you spoken to Pastor Johnson?" Carter asked.

Pastor Johnson had been in the family for three generations of the Charming family now. He was family. And he'd also married Carter to his sweetheart Paige, not too long ago.

"No, I haven't," Cameron replied.

"What's stopping you?"

"Time," he said.

"You've got plenty of it over the holidays, bro."

"Too much time," Cameron grumbled.

"Speaking of which, we need to kick your you know what during the snowball fight."

He grinned. Yes, last year he'd whooped their behind during a snowball charity fundraiser. It was a fun way to raise funds for the Children's new play center and a fun way to get wet in the snow while doing it too. The children had a blast watching the adults make a fool of themselves. And the kids each had their own snowball fun later amongst themselves too. He felt good helping out. But again, the loneliness swept over him like an avalanche once he returned home to his cabin. A place he spent less and less time each year after his family went to be with the Lord.

"It's on, bro," he said, before ending the call.

He continued to drive then he paused for a moment. He reached down to turn on the satellite radio, but the station would be playing Christmas tunes. The stations played all the Christmas songs both new and old, twenty-four hours a day during the month of December. His late wife had always tuned into that channel.

Should he play the songs now?

Would it dampen his mood?

Or would it make him feel closer to her?

He took a chance on the lonely quiet road and reached down to turn on the radio.

"All right, sweetheart. You always said we should play Christmas songs during the month of December," he spoke out loud as if speaking to his late wife. "Well, this one's for you." His voice was a whisper.

The song that came on after the DJ finished talking was *Do You Hear What I Hear?*

Sweet tune.

He and his late wife used to love singing that holiday song together. It was as if they were meant to sing it. It brought back memories that made him feel warm inside.

Just then, after fiddling with the radio station again to get it tuned again, his truck swerved slightly to the right.

Oh, no.

Chapter 5

Cat's eyes were fixed on the back of the cabin.

There was no back door.

How could that be?

It was then she remembered that this was not the original cabin she had selected. She'd changed her mind at the last moment and asked her agent to get a smaller cabin. She'd only seen the pictures over the Internet. She'd never seen it up close until now.

Great.

She heaved a sigh and rubbed her shoulders again trying to keep warm even though she was wearing her winter jacket.

Just then, she thought about her dear grandfather. She hoped he was warm and safe. A lot warmer than she was.

He deserved the best. She remembered when she had seen him at his home in New York, alone not long after Grandma had died. He was having a rough time then. There was no heat in that old house. Eventually, when the lease was up and he expressed he wanted to stay in a nice place with a lot of people just like him, she went with him to tour a few lovely retirement centers. He had worried about the price but she explained to him that she was doing well with her blog and social media page and that she was getting a nice large advance for her new book based on her blog. She assured him that she could take care of anything he needed.

And she meant it. The look on his face at the time melted her heart into a warm place.

She loved him and would do anything for him.

Speaking of which. That's why she had to get this book done this week to send to her agent. The publisher was waiting for her draft. That's what's paying the bills. If she couldn't hand in her draft and get over this block she'd been having in her creativity, she didn't know what would happen to her grandfather—or to her. She had to get this done. She'd already used some of the advance to pay the rent for this small cabin that wouldn't let her inside for some reason.

She held onto the side of the cottage as she carefully walked down the icy snowy side trying hard not to fall.

She had a funny leg as she liked to call it. It acted up sometimes. They did x-rays and ultrasounds and all kinds of tests and couldn't find anything wrong. Doc just told her to be careful. Sometimes the body acted up for no reason.

Well, she hoped it wouldn't do so now.

As she pressed her boot into the snow, hoping to have some sort of grip, she felt the ice move beneath her.

Oh, no. No, no, no, no, no.

She overstretched the muscle on the back of her lower leg, and...

Kaboom!

She slipped and tumbled down the sloping side of the cabin.

Oh, no. Please don't act up again, she pleaded with her left leg. *Please don't let me down now.*

Too late.

She went down like a sack of hay.

Her funny leg let her down, yet again. And on a night like this where she was all alone. Outside. Just her and the elements near a secluded cabin—just as she'd asked for. The saying flew into her mind.

Be careful what you ask for because you just might get it.

Intense pain swept through her body. A heavy ache twisted through her.

She fell and hurt herself on the ice.

She started to fade out.

The snowy night began to fade into a darkness.

Her eyelids became heavy...

Chapter 6

Cameron's detour ended up turning onto another side street. He was about to turn his truck around but for some reason he decided to drive further down the road, looking at the nice Christmas lights on some of the cabins.

All of the cabins had pretty decorations on them. Well, most of them. It was like a winter wonderland.

As he continued to drive down the street he noticed something in the distance. An isolated cabin. Cameron squinted as he slowed down his truck and looked through his windshield. He thought he saw something under the streetlight outside a cabin on the right. But he must be imagining it.

There was something on the front lawn.

Just then it moved.

Aw, man. That's a person.

He wondered what that fella was doing out on the ground in the middle of a snowstorm and on a cold night like tonight. Was the person drunk or something?

Maybe the Lord brought Cameron down this road for a reason.

He slowed down his truck and stopped the engine. He then pulled his coat on and adjusted his cowboy hat. He got out of the truck and slammed the door shut.

"Excuse me," he called out. "Need some help?"

He was taught in one of his emergency preparedness workshops to always ask if a person needed help. Never assume unless it's obvious or they could not speak for themselves.

He'd once thought a guy was attacking a woman in a park and went over there and grabbed the guy by his collar. Big mistake. The couple were newlywed and playing some sort of game, having fun. It didn't seem like it at the time. But he'd learned his lesson. Still, it looked obvious this fella on the ground needed help. He was practically down in the snow. And it didn't look as if he was making a snow angel either.

"I can't get up," the voice sounded. But it wasn't a man's voice. It was a beautiful soft voice of a woman.

"Ma'am, I'm right here," he said, moving closer to her. It was then that he saw her wavy shiny hair tucked under her hood. She was on her side. She turned her head to face him.

Her lovely eyes stared into his and his heart turned over in his chest.

"Are you hurt?" he asked, reaching for her.

"My leg. It just cramped up." She managed to turn over and reached for him and hugged her arms around his neck as he pulled her up.

He carefully assessed her movements to make sure she could get up safely. The sweet scent of her perfume wafted to his nose as the breeze blew around them. She smelled like an angel. Her fragrance was intoxicating and pleasing to his senses. He shifted his thoughts again. Why was he thinking of Ms. Beauty and her scent at a time like this? What was with this cowboy?

"Are you sure it's not broken? Did you fall?"

"No. I didn't fall that hard. I just slipped on the side slope there. The back of my leg hurts."

"You might've pulled your hamstring, Ma'am," he said. "Just let me carry you. You'll be all right. We need to get you inside."

She hopped as she walked with him. He was leading her to the cabin.

"Is this your place?"

"Yes."

"Good. Let's get you inside."

She stopped walking and she sighed deeply. She stared wordlessly at the cabin.

"You okay?" he asked gently, following her gaze.

Her eyes were so pretty. Long thick lashes framed her beautiful eyes. Her lips were shapely and red like strawberries. Her cheekbones high and defined. She was breathtaking.

Just then a recognition struck him.

"Cat?" he asked.

She looked into his eyes and the look of surprise filled her pretty face.

"Cameron?" she said.

It had been years since he'd seen her. Not since high school.

"Well look at that," he said. "Fancy seeing you again."

Relief washed over her. "I am so glad it's someone I know. I was worried about being found by a stranger." She chuckled.

He grinned. Just then something filled him inside. A warm feeling.

He remembered Cat from high school. They'd even dated once but then her folks died in some freak accident. It was horrible. He remembered how brave she was. He'd reached out to her then but at the time he was only a high school student and didn't know too much about emotional support.

Her grandparents took her in and she'd moved to New York with them where they'd moved from Mistletoe.

Gosh, he'd missed her then.

But then he got on with his life and they never did keep in touch. He'd married, of course. And the last he'd heard was that she'd found someone in New York.

"Yes, what a surprise. Thank you for saving me out there. Never knew I'd see you again. Of course, we are in a small town but I was supposed to be spending time in this cabin for the month."

"Really?"

"Yes, I'm working on a book. I have a contract."

"A book? Congratulations!" He was always so proud of her. From the time he'd known her she'd always had her nose in a book. He'd admired her intellect back when they were in high school. He still couldn't get over seeing her again.

"Thanks."

"Well, you'd better get inside where it's warmer than out here," he said.

"I can't go inside," she told him.

"Why not?"

"The door won't let me."

He was confused about what she was talking about.

"The door won't *let* you?"

"Wrong key," she finally said. She reached into her purse and took out a bronze key.

"How did that happen?" he asked.

"My agent arranged for me to rent this cabin for a short time. He also got creative and gave me the wrong key. I guess he wanted to test my survival skills." She shook her head and grinned.

He liked her sense of humor. But this wasn't funny one bit. What kind of an agent would give a lady the wrong key to the door of her rented home?

"Okay. Well, right now, we have to get you out of the cold. You'll need to have a doctor look at that leg of yours to be sure you're okay."

"I know what it is."

"You do?"

"Yes," she said. "It happens once in a while."

"Talk about timing," he said.

"I know, right?"

He felt comfortable around her and could tell the feeling was mutual. It was as if time hadn't passed between them.

Just then she gave him a look of concern. Or was that sympathy?

"Something wrong?" he asked.

"Oh, no. It's been a while since I've been here. I read about your family. Oh gosh, Cameron, I am so sorry about your wife and stepdaughter. I'd sent some flowers when I heard."

His heart twisted in his chest.

He could only imagine what she must be thinking. She'd lost her own parents in a freak accident too.

Guilt and pain swept through his body leaving him numb and broken about his now late wife and stepdaughter—once again. He wished he'd been there to save them.

"Thank you." His voice was soft. He hoped she didn't hear the pain in his tone and the sorrow that he was feeling once again now. "I'm thankful to have my family help me get through this. Not just my church family but my extended family."

"Of course. During a time like that it's hard to get through grief without the support of family, friends and the church."

His family was well known in the town of Mistletoe. They owned the largest ranch in the district and had many community events going on. The Charming Ranch had been in the family since the late 1800s. Their great-grandfather was one of the earlier settlers when the town was new.

"So, you write a blog?" he asked, trying to change the subject. He didn't want to go down that painful road again right now.

"Yes. I write a woman's blog," she said, proudly. "I also get into some news stuff once in a while."

Interest in her blog piqued him. He'd always admired writers and authors. Being able to create stories to entertain and enlighten people was a spectacular gift. Writers shared stories that helped make sense of human behavior, about living and having dreams and about love.

His late wife had always loved reading blogs and listening to podcasts. She loved learning about people, learning about life. He missed her like crazy.

"I was wondering if I could ask you a favor," she said.

"What is it?" He wanted to help her. It was as if he wanted to do for her what he did not, could not do for his wife.

Was that why his path was directed down this road tonight? He had no idea why he continued to drive down this lonely path. Did the man upstairs have something to do with it? To help him re-write history somehow. To give him another chance?

No. It couldn't be. It just had to be a coincidence, right?

"I need you to force the door open or...see if you can get the window open," she said, regretfully.

He stopped for a minute. "You want me to break in and enter?"

"Yes. I mean no, of course not. I'm on the lease for the month." She looked apologetically. "I already paid up for the month."

He grinned and arched a brow. "Now how do I know you're telling me the truth?"

Chapter 7

"You're right. What was I thinking asking you that?" Cat placed her hands on her hips and sighed. "I could be pulling the wool over your eyes."

He sighed. "From the moment I met you in high school, you've always been an honest girl. Always doing the right thing. I don't doubt you for a minute," he said. "But there must be another way in."

"Really?" she asked as the cold winter wind blew around them.

He stood there looking deep into her eyes and her tummy did the butterflies thing.

Oh, my goodness.

He was more gorgeous than she'd remembered. Beautiful eyes and cheekbones that looked like they could dodge ice pellets.

And he had something her recent ex never had.

Integrity.

A warm feeling swept through her belly over Cameron, the tall, dark and handsome cowboy before her. And his cologne. What was that earthy beautiful scent? It was scrumptious.

Man, this cowboy was a true hero. An honest one too. A noble spirit. The do-the-right-thing type of cowboy. He not only stopped and turned around to help her before he knew who she was. But he had scruples too.

Cameron never changed being the sweet guy he'd always been.

Stop that, Cat.

You've sworn off dating, remember? You cannot get attracted to this cowboy in shining armour. Focus. Focus on your goals. You don't need any more handsome distractions after your ex.

She fought to sweep away her feelings of attraction to this cowboy, the guy she'd fallen in love with in high school. Of course, they'd grown apart. After her parents passed away and she moved to New York with her grandparents, they never did keep in touch. He'd also left town. This was way before texting and social media were popular. And by the time she'd moved to New York, it was too painful to keep in touch with anyone from Mistletoe at the time. It only brought back sad memories of losing her parents there.

"I know," she said feeling hopeless. "There must be another way in."

That was Cameron for you. Always the optimist. But she didn't feel too optimistic right now. Right now, she felt the bone chill of the wind on this wintery night.

If she could use her cell phone, she could have called her agent. She'd programmed his phone number into her phone and always used speed dial so she didn't have it by memory.

She had to admit it, as desperate as she felt right now to get inside to her warm cabin out from the cold windy winter night, she liked Cameron's stance. Find another way.

She was just so desperate that she hadn't realized that she couldn't ask someone to break into a cabin she was renting. What was she thinking?

Oh, right. Her brain was frozen right now.

That's it. She had brain freeze. Or common sense freeze.

The temperature seemed to plummet with each minute outside. She hugged herself to keep warm, rubbing her arms, wishing she'd worn her thicker Parka jacket.

"You want to sit in my truck and keep warm?"

"Nah, I'm good, thanks. Let's just figure out how to get inside."

He glanced at the large suitcase near the front door.

"So you moved back to work on your book."

"Yes. Just for the month. I'm so thankful to have this contract. I share my apartment in New York with some roommates. I needed a quiet space so I thought I'd move back and work on the book."

"That's smart of you. You were always so dedicated to whatever you set your heart on."

The words of encouragement brought a slither of joy to her heart. Her ex, her recent ex never said anything kind or sweet like that to her. What had she missed out on all these years?

Still, a gnawing feeling grabbed her.

Stay away from this sweet cowboy, Cat. You have no room in your life for relationships. Not anymore. Look at what happened with your recent ex.

She had to focus and not get too caught up on the holiday mood or feelings for Cameron. He was her past.

Besides, she just didn't seem to have much luck with men. After her recent ex broke her heart, she'd been so down for days, she didn't think she could get out of that funk and write again. There was no way she was going to take a chance on anything messing with her head—again.

"Thank you. I need to make sure the draft is ready by Christmas. It's what's paying my bills and taking care of my grandfather."

"That's so nice of you. How is he doing?"

"Thanks for asking. He's doing well." She blew out a puff of air.

"Listen, why don't you call your agent and let him know what's going on. Maybe he could get you the key."

"Good idea except I don't have any juice left on my phone and his number's programmed on it. I don't know it by heart—unfortunately."

"Oh, right. That sucks. Sorry to hear that."

"No worries, it's not your fault my battery's dead and I didn't memorize his number. Hey, you have your phone with you right?"

Silly question. Everyone had their phone with them. It was a part of who they were nowadays. But the question was, did he have enough battery power left on his phone to make a call?

Just then his phone rang, a melody sounded over the speaker. It was Away in a Manger.

She arched her brow. Interesting ring tone. She'd never heard anyone have that as a ring tone before. Cameron was a one of a kind sentimental cowboy.

"What's wrong?" he asked, answering his phone and telling the person he'd be with them soon.

"Oh, nothing. Did you change your ring tone to a Christmas song?" she asked. "Please tell me you don't have that song playing all year round?"

"Nope. Just for Christmas. I take it you're not into the Christmas spirit?"

She looked around. "Definitely not this year."

He took his call after excusing himself as they stood on her porch waiting for goodness knew what.

When he was finished, he turned to her.

"I've got some bad news."

"Oh, no. What's wrong?"

The last thing she needed now was bad news. What could be worse than what's happening now?

Chapter 8

Cameron was mesmerized by Cat's beauty, but he tried to stay focused. He liked her spunk and her energy but she was only here for the month and besides, he wasn't interested in pursuing anything.

He thought about the upcoming Barn Hall Dance. His folks had been onto him to bring a date but there was no way he would ask Cat. Besides, she was busy and he didn't want to date again.

"There's a weather warning in town," he continued. "Mayor's advising everyone to stay indoors."

"Oh, no."

"Yeah, I know the irony, right? But my brother works down at the town hall. He's heading home now. You'd better let me get you somewhere warm."

"I need to stay here. I don't have any family here. Not anymore."

"I see," he said. "Well you can always stay at my family ranch. You know that won't be any trouble. They'd love to see you again."

"That's very kind of you to offer, Cameron but I don't want to put you all out. I mean, it's not like we've been in touch all these years."

"Hey, you know it's no trouble. Our families go way back."

She smiled. Her smile was the prettiest he'd seen in a long time. There was something captivating about Cat. Something about her that resonated with him. Something familiar.

He just felt comfortable around her but he had to ignore those feelings. He was doing what any cowboy would do. He was helping this nice lady out—his high school friend whom he'd shared a date with once while they were students. He had to keep things in perspective.

They both knew that in a small town people knew each other and each other's business and nobody wanted to be the talk of the town. Not that he cared much if people thought he was seeing his high school friend or ex-girlfriend.

Mistletoe was also known for its breathtaking Christmas decorations and festive events at this time of the year, as well as its heavy snowstorms and blizzards. Still, he wanted to make sure she was safe.

"I just want to make sure you're going to be all right. You know my family's ranch. There are plenty of rooms in the main house. My mother would be happy to have you as a guest."

"Thank you. I'd love to," she said, looking around frantically. "But I really want to be here. I must get into my cabin tonight."

He adjusted his cowboy hat.

"Tell you what. Why don't we have a look around," he said as the heavy winds howled around them.

"What do you mean?"

"I mean," he said, looking around the outside of the cabin. "I'm sure the agent didn't just leave you high and dry."

He leaned down beside a rock. He grinned.

"What do you see?" she asked.

"You wouldn't believe it."

Chapter 9

"It's an envelope. That's what you found?" Cat asked incredulously. "My agent left me a letter under a *rock*?" She threw up her hands in disbelief. "What if someone else found it?"

Cat gently took the note that Cameron handed to her.

"Well, the good news is that it was well hidden," Cameron said. "And in this storm, I doubt anyone would even come around here looking for anything."

"True."

"And look on the bright side," he added. "At least it was under a rock, so the wind couldn't blow it away."

She glanced up at the tall, handsome cowboy. She'd almost forgotten how gorgeous he was. He always had the dreamiest set of eyes she'd ever seen on a man. And he had an air of optimism around him. Gorgeous inside and outside. Why didn't they ever get together or made it a point to stay in touch all these years?

He's the one that got away.

She couldn't help but notice his broad shoulders and tall physique. He must be around six feet four inches. A whole foot taller than she stood.

She felt the envelope and noticed there was something inside it.

She tore it open and found a note with a key attached.

She grinned and shook her head in disbelief.

That's Tom for you.

Tom was her agent and her old school friend. He was a part time agent and didn't have any other clients. He just had a love for literature and a few connections in the publishing world. He was an eccentric guy who sometimes did things in an unconventional way. He was also a part time real estate agent. He'd told her that hustling was the name of the game.

She read the note and chuckled.

"Everything okay?" he asked.

"I guess it should be now," she said. "Tom, my agent, left me this note saying he was sorry he sent me the wrong key. He also sold a cottage around here. He sells homes on the side. I guess he sold this cabin too as an investment for someone who wanted to rent it out. So I guess, I have the other customer's key and she or he has mine."

"He sells homes *and* manuscripts. Interesting," he said. "You might want to get the lock changed then," Cameron offered.

"Good thinking. I'll ask him if the new owners don't mind seeing as someone else could have the key to their cabin."

She tried the lock with the key from the envelope and nothing happened at first.

"You might want to give it a good wiggle, sometimes new locks take a little time to get in smoothly," Cameron said.

"I just hope he cut the right key this time," she said, hopefully.

She tried again and sure enough, it worked!

A wave of relief washed over Cat.

"Yay! We're in." She held out her hands as if welcoming her new home for the month.

"You mean you're in." He grinned.

"Well, you know what? We're a team now, aren't we?"

"I'll help you inside," he said, "Hold on to my shoulder."

Cameron grabbed her luggage with one hand and then held her carefully with his other free hand.

Her luggage was heavy—at least to her. It seemed like Cameron had no trouble holding it, like he was holding a feather pillow.

"Thank you," she said and held on to his firm shoulder. The cowboy looked as if he bench-pressed two hundred pounds of weight every day. He was fit as a horse.

He helped her into the foyer of her cozy new cabin as she hobbled on one foot.

"How's the pain, Cat?" he asked.

"Still there but it's getting better, thank the Lord. I just need to sit down."

"Sure, let me help you." He helped her to the couch where she sat down.

"Thank you so much," she said.

"Hey, no worries."

He then glanced around the cabin. "Nice cabin. I see its fully furnished."

"Yes, that was the deal. My agent said he'd have everything ready with new furniture fit for a writer in residence, so to speak. And he was right."

She looked around, pleased. There was a fireplace, a lovely rug in the center of the cabin's living room, a comfy chair and a couch with three square pillows, just in case she wanted to lie down and write. The hardwood floors shined like marble. The open-concept kitchen area had new cabinets. And the large windows gave her a nice view of the outside.

"Your agent sure did a good job."

"He did. I must remember to thank him later. And forgive him. Or maybe he should forgive *me*."

"For what?"

"For all those awful things I was thinking about him when I was locked outside of the cabin." She chuckled, shaking her head.

Cameron grinned.

"How could I ever thank you?" she asked her former high school friend, the cowboy who rescued her tonight.

"It's no problem. Really," he said.

She paused for a moment to ponder.

"Something on your mind?" he asked, gently.

"Yes. How did you find me?" she asked curiously.

He adjusted his cowboy hat. She loved when he did that. There was just something about a man in a cowboy hat, wearing a thick jacket, leather boots and jeans that mesmerized her.

He sighed.

"You wouldn't believe it," he said.

"Oh? Try me."

He grinned. "I'll tell you in a moment after we get you settled in here."

"Okay. You promise you won't forget."

"When it comes to you, Cat. I wouldn't forget anything."

She then glanced into Cameron's beautiful eyes then looked away as her heart fluttered in her chest.

She hoped he wouldn't see the rouge on her cheeks. She could tell she was blushing. Heat climbed to her cheeks. How could she still have feelings for Cameron? He was her past. She wasn't doing this.

"You know, I was thinking about your ring tone," she said, trying to change the subject as fast as she could.

"What about it?" he asked.

"Do you remember when we were in the Nativity Play at Christmas in grade nine?"

He smiled. And that cute dimple appeared on his cheeks just as it did in high school. She was always mesmerized by his charming smile but she tried not to glance at it now. Why did she bring up that Christmas play?

"You played Mary and I played Joseph," he said.

"Yes, I'll never forget that. I fumbled for my lines. I was so nervous."

"You were just perfect," he said.

He was very kind, she thought. She thought they always got along well together. Did she think he was too nice for her—just friend material back then. Well, she certainly didn't think so now but she was determined to brush that feeling aside. The feeling of comfort and familiarity with a nice old friend from her past. A guy in high school she'd once dated. A nice guy who was always so serious and focused on helping out on his family's ranch and looking after his younger siblings. He was everything her recent ex was not.

"I think we should take a look at your leg," he said, changing the subject.

Was there an awkward pause between them just now? Was that why he rushed to change the subject? It was for the best anyway. She didn't know why her mind went down memory lane just now. Her leg was the part of her that needed attention.

"Where does it hurt?" he asked her. "Can I touch here?"

"Sure" she said, swallowing hard.

"Does it hurt when I press there?"

The touch of his soft skin on hers, made her heart jump all over the place and butterflies in her tummy exploded.

No, this is wrong. I no longer have feelings for Cameron. He's my friend from my high school days. Nothing more.

Was she trying hard to convince herself?

"Uh, no. Yes. I mean, no."

"You sure?"

"Try there." She pointed to the spot behind her leg as she rested her foot on the empty stone coffee table in front of the couch.

He touched that to see if it hurt and she said just a little.

"Well," he said, after examining her leg. "You'll need to apply RICE."

"Rice?" she asked, perplexed.

"You know," he said, 'the acronym for rice: rest the injured muscle, ice the injured part to reduce any kind of swelling, compress the area, elevate the injured leg."

"Oh, right. RICE," she said, remembering her First Aid course she took years ago. "Of course."

Like seriously. How would she remember that acronym if she never had to use it. Okay, well, he was right about that.

"You can also take an Advil if that will help."

"You know what," she said. "It will subside. Actually, it's getting better."

He smiled. "You sure about that?"

He had no idea. But his presence was oddly comforting and relaxing—just as it had been in the past. She liked his aura and everything about his calm yet take-charge demeanor.

After he made sure her leg was stable on the table, he asked her if he could make her something to drink.

"That would be nice. I'm not sure if Tom stocked the fridge."

"I'll go see."

"Thank you." She touched his hand when he got up, not meaning to. The delightful feeling sent shivers dancing down her back.

Why was she reacting to this handsome cowboy like that?

She had to keep her mind focused on her work. There was no time for relationships. No time for dating. Not for the foreseeable future.

Still, she was grateful the good Lord sent an angel in disguise in her path when she was down on her face, *literally*, in the snow.

She was glad it was a good Samaritan, a church-going cowboy who spotted her first in the dark. Her beloved friend from high school. She was glad he spotted her when he did while driving down that lonely road at that time of night.

When he got back from the kitchen, he brought her a cup of steaming hot chocolate.

"Looks like Tom had you all stocked up nicely for your writing marathon."

She smiled appreciatively. "Thank you. And thank you for everything again. I don't want you to be waiting on me hand and foot. I'm sure you have places to go."

"I do, but I want to make sure you're all right first. You can barely weight bear on your one leg."

"I know," she agreed, reluctantly. "Why don't you make yourself some hot chocolate? Or would you prefer coffee?"

"I'm good, thanks," he said. "Just want to make sure you're okay."

He got up.

"What are you looking for?" she asked.

"A phone, a charger, an outlet. You need to have things close by to you so you won't have to get up all the time."

He began to arrange some of the furniture within safe and close distance to her.

"Do you need to lie down? What if you need to go to bed after I leave?"

"I'm sure the bedroom isn't far from here. I think it's just down the hall from what I remember from seeing the layout."

"Do you want me to take you there now?' he asked.

"Actually, the couch is really cozy," she said leaning into it. Just then her leg ached mercilessly again. A sharp pain then shot through her leg at the back.

Cameron was right. She wouldn't do too well on her own right now. What if she fell if she tried to get up?

What would she do then?

He placed her phone charger next to her and began to charge her phone.

Man, he was so considerate. Her recent ex was nothing like Cameron. Once, when she'd sprained her wrist, he didn't even show any sense of concern, not like Cameron.

"You want me to start the fire in the fireplace?" he asked, helpfully.

"Actually, that would be nice. But do you have all the things you need?"

He grinned. "There's wood by the side there. Looks like Tom had you all set up."

She smiled. "Sorry, I might be from the small town but I identify as a city girl. And I wouldn't know a fireplace starter if I saw one."

"It's all right. Glad to help."

He paused for a moment. I'm going to show you how to set this up, and what to do when the wood is finished burning."

"Sounds like a plan," she said.

"Just wait here a minute," he said, softly.

"Why? Where are you going?"

"Just making sure the chimney's open."

After everything was set up, Cameron made sure safety was in place.

"You are a true hero," she said. "I can't thank you enough."

She realized she sounded like a broken record repeating herself over and over. She just hadn't been around a man like that who was so helpful. Her recent ex certainly wasn't. She just wanted Cameron to know that she really appreciated what he was doing for her. What would she have done all alone out there injured in the snow on a cold night like tonight?

"You know something," she said. "It was really good of you to stop and reach out to me while I was lying flat on the snow."

"Aww, it's nothing. Any man would have done the same."

"No, I'm afraid not."

"What do you mean?" he asked, genuinely puzzled.

"My ex, the guy I was dating in New York, wouldn't have stopped. We were walking in the town once and there was a guy who looked homeless lying down flat on his face."

"Oh, no. Did you check to see if he was all right?" Cameron asked, concerned.

"Well, I did. I told my ex, whom I will not mention his name," she said, shaking her head. "I told him we should go and see if the man's all right."

"And? What did he say?"

"I won't use his words but he wasn't very kind about it and said he was probably intoxicated to put it lightly. I tried to call out to the man to see if he was all right. He looked as if he was having some sort of crisis. At the end of the day, he's a human being. And no one knows why a person ends up in the place they do," she said.

"Good on you," Cameron said.

She really felt Cameron's warm sentiment. This cowboy was all heart.

"So I took out my cell phone while my ex walked on, and I called the emergency."

"Atta girl."

"Thanks. It turned out that the man had a stroke and paramedics got there in time. I just shiver to think of what would've happened if no one had stopped. I should have seen my ex was no good at the time. We didn't last much longer after that. Don't get me wrong, it wasn't just that incident, it was other things I'd noticed. He'd just finished college and was on his way with his career and..." She stopped.

She could tell Cameron wanted to hear more. She didn't want to tell him that she'd caught her ex cheating on her with some dancer—a former college classmate in the Dancing Arts program.

"I'm sorry, I don't mean to babble on."

"You're not babbling, Cat. It's okay to get things off your chest."

Validation. He was validating me. He has no idea what that means to me. But I will not get too caught up in that. He's a good friend. An old friend from high school. Someone I appreciate and I don't want to get ahead of myself or risk messing things up between us.

"Thank you," she said, appreciatively. "What would I have done without you, tonight?"

He grinned. "Just get well and share your book with the world," he said.

Man, Cameron was so nice. It was refreshing to be around a guy like that.

Her phone pinged. The battery was slowly charging it. It had some power in it now. At least 1% and counting.

"I really appreciate you doing that for me. Can't believe my phone was completely dead."

"It'll be fine soon. Shouldn't take too long to charge. It's happened to me before too while on the road all day."

"I find that hard to believe," she said. "You seem so organized."

He grinned and his boyish grin produced a cute dimple on his cheek. He was adorable. Charming. In other words, he lived up to his last name. She knew the Charming brothers and their small-town charm. They were strong cowboys with a heart of gold.

"Actually, you'd be surprised when you're busy running errands all day," he said.

"Speaking of which, were you running errands when you drove down this road?" she asked him.

"Actually no. You'd be surprised. Coming down this road wasn't planned." He then grinned and looked up towards the ceiling of the cabin for a split second. "Well, at least not by me."

She smiled and agreed. "I think someone's looking out for me."

"You better believe that. I was driving and intended to turn one direction but my truck took me down here. And when I tried to turn around something told me not to."

"It was meant to be," she said.

"Looks like the man upstairs wanted us to cross paths this evening."

"Yes, it sure looks like it," she said. "You know I'm going to church on Christmas morning. I haven't been in months but I will this year."

"In months? How come?"

"I don't celebrate Christmas. Not anymore. My grandfather is my only surviving close relative now and he doesn't either."

"I'm sorry to hear that."

"It's okay. Anyway, we vowed to never get hung up on the holiday celebrations again after Grandma passed."

"I can see it must be difficult for you. But you something, I think you'd feel different with the Christmas spirit if you give it another chance.."

"You think so?"

"Yes."

"Do you still celebrate it...?"

He looked down for a moment. "Yes, I do now. I have to."

"You *have* to?" She arched a brow.

"Yes. My wife and stepdaughter used to celebrate it with me. And after they passed," he said, emotion in his voice.

He stared into the fireplace. The orange flames created a nice glow on his face.

Cat wanted to reach out and hug him. Her heart broke for what he'd been through. She could not imagine what it must be like. He'd lost so much, yet he had so much to be thankful for.

"I decided," he continued, "to carry on the things that made them happy when they were here. Actually, things that made us all happy. It's a way to not just bring the spirit of the holiday around but their memories as well."

"That's so noble of you," she said, softly.

"Just doing the right thing," he said.

"So were you celebrating tonight?" she asked, wanting to know more. She wanted to help him celebrate it. Even though she hadn't done so in many years.

"Well, I was at the children's center at the hospital volunteering and bringing Christmas gifts for the kids there."

"I think that's wonderful of you," she said.

"Hey, I've got some spare time now. Besides, we're always looking for volunteers. Not everyone has the time. We even have this center for creative expression for teens having trouble with expressing their feelings."

"Oh, my goodness. I would love to help out but I don't know if I'd have time," she said regretfully.

"Hey, no worries. Of course, you'll be working on your book."

"If I finish early, I'll let you know," she said, hopefully.

"That sounds good! That would be amazing if you could take part in the creative writing therapy workshops."

"I'm sure it would."

A feeling of dread swept over her. She was never going to see her old friend, this handsome and caring cowboy, again after tonight. They'd probably go their separate ways and lose touch again as they had in the past. She knew she was going to be busy focusing on her book and then, by Christmas, she'd be back in New York.

Just then, they were inches from each other and she thought he was about to kiss her. Was he going to kiss her?

A second later, he pulled away.

That had to be her imagination. Why would he want to kiss her when they'd only just become re-acquainted after all these years?

Silly girl.

How embarrassing.

"So how's your book coming along?" he asked, probably trying to change the mood.

"Well, it's practically finished. I just have to go through the draft and make sure to tweak it and add some editorial changes. The final draft is due very soon. I'm so thankful I can take care of Grandpa with the money from my work."

"You're a real trooper, you know that?" he said.

"I try. Family is everything," she added.

"I like the way you think." He looked as if he were deep in thought for a moment.

"Are you okay?" she asked, trying to pretend she didn't try to kiss him earlier.

"I'm good. You're right though. Family is everything."

She could kick herself.

He'd lost *his* family. Why, oh, why did she bring it up?

She hoped one day, he'd be able to move forward despite the pain of losing his wife and child and find some form of happiness later.

Cat thought about that for a moment. She had lost so much in her life as well. So many people in so many ways, but she always created a wall around her heart to distance herself.

Just then a thought struck her.

Could she ask this caring and charismatic cowboy one last favor?

Chapter 10

"Could I ask you another favor?" Cat asked, her pretty eyes wide and charming. "I know I don't deserve it."

"What makes you say that?"

She was humble as warm apple pie, yet so beautiful and acted as if she didn't know it. He was mesmerized by her beauty, her spirit, her aura. He'd never felt this way about any woman since his wife passed. He never thought he ever would again.

"I don't know," she said. "You've done more than enough for me."

"Try me."

"Would you like to help me decorate this cozy little cabin?" Cat said, with a cute innocent expression on her face.

"You're having a change of heart?"

"Well, I almost died out there in the snow if it weren't for the good Lord bringing you into my path. I think it would be nice to get back into putting up festive decorations to celebrate the true meaning of the season. It's the very least I could do."

He found her absolutely charming. Adorable.

And just a moment ago, he felt a pulse between them. Their faces, their lips were so close and he wanted to kiss her. But he couldn't. He wouldn't. It was just the passing moment. That's all it was. She was his former high school girlfriend, a good friend from the past. Nothing more.

He didn't want to think about getting involved with another woman. Not now. Maybe never.

Though, he had to admit, this was the first time he'd ever felt so close to a woman, since his wife went to be with the Lord.

This was the first time in a long while he'd felt so comfortable, so wanted, so secure for some reason.

Was the man upstairs trying to tell him something? Show him a sign?

He'd heard of instant attraction before. Kismet. He just didn't believe in it. And he'd dated Cat in high school but this was different. More intense. Still, he didn't want to get his hopes up.

If he thought about it, he had been devastated since his wife and child died, that he wasn't able to save them. So, now, even though this situation wasn't the same thing, not even close, he was able to save someone else from danger.

Was this the reason he was brought down this lonely road? He had to admit it was perfect timing. Cat could have frozen to death out there on the cold night if he hadn't gotten there in time. Her leg had seized up. That had happened to him once and it took him hours for his leg to feel all right to move.

What if she'd been there for hours in the frigid temperature?

He tried not to think about that but just thanked the Lord he was there in time.

She was special.

There was just something about her aura that connected to him in a beautiful way. He hoped to see her again before she went back to New York.

"So, you've got the Christmas spirit back, have you?" he asked with a grin.

"You'd better believe it, cowboy. How about it?"

Her smile was wide and beautiful.

"Sure, why not?"

Chapter 11

Cat

The following week, after Cat had time to settle into her cabin and get some writing done, she took a stroll through the Mistletoe Market with Cameron to hunt for some Christmas decorations. What was she doing? She shouldn't be having fun with her ex from high school. She should be getting ready to go back to New York. But she just couldn't help herself. It was just like the old days. Spending quality time with the one you feel good about.

Cameron had been so sweet to her over the past week, making sure she had enough wood for her fireplace and making sure her fridge and cupboards were stocked with enough food to last her for the duration of her stay.

"You really don't have to," she'd told him.

"Hey, it's no trouble," he'd said, casually.

For the first time she had a chance to be Cat. It was a change having someone look out for her instead of the other way around.

With her ex, she was always making sure he was okay and making sure he had his assignments done because she wanted to see him succeed. And for what? For him to turn around and break her heart?

She didn't want to fill her mind with her recent ex right now. She had to get rid of that habit.

Count your blessings, not your troubles.

That's what her grandfather always told her and she was going to practice doing that from now on. It was so easy to do whenever she was around Cameron. He had that special aura around him.

They picked up gold ornaments for her Christmas tree at her cabin and later went to the tree lot to pick out a small tree.

Later, Cameron had helped her set it all up. They had a ball of fun in each other's company. He had such a fine sense of humor. She regretted that she didn't work harder to keep in touch—before he got married, of course.

**

"Where's Cat?" the friendly voice on the other end of the phone asked with a chuckle later that afternoon. "What happened to her?"

"Grandpa, it's me," Cat answered, cheerfully.

"I know, darling. I was only pulling your leg. You just sound like a different person."

"I do?"

"You seem more relaxed. Cheerful. You sound like my granddaughter again. So, who is the lucky guy?"

She playfully rolled her eyes and grinned as she pressed the phone to her right ear.

"Very funny, Grandpa." She sat by the window with her laptop open and peered out at the lovely snow-covered lake behind her cabin.

The town was blanketed in a lovely coat of white. The pine trees capped with snow. Everything seemed so light for a change. She really liked the cozy atmosphere of Mistletoe. A huge change from her life in the city.

"What makes you think it's about a guy?" she asked him.

"Because you sound like you're in love."

A warm feeling slid over her at that thought followed by a wave of anxiety.

No, it couldn't be. She swore she would never enter into a relationship again. Not for now. She was going to focus on her career for a change. Focus on Cat.

Sure, she was having a wonderful time with Cameron in Mistletoe but he was her friend from high school, a cowboy from a small town and she was a city girl from the big city.

Her life was in New York now. The last time she'd dropped everything for a guy, it had backfired on her. Never again.

She sighed deeply. "I was locked out of my cabin and this really nice cowboy helped me out. We're just friends. Nothing more. Nothing will come of it, Grandpa."

"Locked out of your cabin?" her grandfather sounded alarmed.

"Oh, no, I'm fine. Thanks to Cameron. He spotted me in the snow and..." She bit down on her lower lip. She didn't want to tell him too much to get him worried. "I'm fine though. It all worked out. And Cameron and I got back to talking. You remember Cameron."

"Oh, right. The Charmings' boy. A fine young man he is. So sad about his late wife and stepdaughter."

"I know. A horrible tragedy."

"How is he coping?"

"He's doing as best as he could. I was so glad we met up again though."

"So am I. You two always did get along together. I remember you would write about him when you were in high school."

A grin curved her lips. She did write about him back then, didn't she?

"Oh, come on now," her grandfather said. "It's a sign."

"A sign?"

"Yes, it's a sign to move on. Maybe you two could..."

"Grandpa," she said lovingly, before he could get to finish. She didn't want to get her hopes up for nothing—or his. "It's not like that."

"How do you know? You know sometimes the good Lord directs our steps. We need to open our eyes and our hearts."

She swallowed hard. She knew her grandfather was right. But the trouble was, she was afraid. Afraid of getting hurt again.

***

Carter

A couple more weeks had passed by and Cameron and Cat ended up decorating her small cabin while she worked on her manuscript. She'd told him that she had writer's block until they met and now she felt at ease to write.

They even spent time at the Children's Hospital and Cat had given the teens some fun writing exercises to do. They loved her. And he could see the love on her face. She would be great with her own kids if she ever became a mother.

He had no idea why he thought that but he just did.

They went out to dinner at the Mistletoe Steak House and later spent time shopping for ornaments at the Christmas market. They even had a few fun snow fights and built a snowman together.

By the week before Christmas, Cat told him she had to go back to the New York to her apartment and hand in her manuscript.

She would be gone. Just like the feelings of joy he'd had over the past few weeks with her.

Her cabin was just a temporary setup. He'd hoped she would want to stay in Mistletoe, the town she grew up in, but he understood.

"So you're leaving for good?" he asked, as they rode horses at the Charming Ranch. He'd taken her on a trail ride and she loved the ranch.

"I have to. It's been great here, but...I don't belong in a small town. Not anymore"

"What makes you say that?"

"I'm a city girl at heart. Don't get me wrong, it's nice and quiet here, but..." She sighed as the horse continued to move on the trail.

"I was hoping you'd come to the Charming Ranch Barn Hall Christmas Dance."

"Oh, I've heard about that. The Annual Barn Hall Dance, right?"

"That's right?"

"I have a flight out tonight. I'm going to see Grandpa on Christmas Day and then...I guess work on my next book and my New Year's blog."

"Of course." He tried to hide his disappointment. But he admired her for her work.

"You brought the spirit of the holidays back and I'm so grateful for you. For that and for saving my life out there."

Saving her life.

He'd saved her life, hadn't he? Hearing her say it brought something inside his heart. It lightened the burden he'd been carrying—even if just a little. He guessed their paths were just meant to cross briefly before going back to their own lives. She received the spirit of the holidays and he received a way to forgive himself. A gift they could not deny was a miracle.

But sadly, it looked as if their moment was about to end. Would he ever see her again?

Chapter 12

Cameron

"You look miserable today son," Cameron's mother said to him at the main house. "What happened? You were so happy these past few weeks."

"I know," he said, not realizing his tone was low until it was too late. "Cat's going back to New York."

"Oh, I'm so sorry to hear that."

"Yeah, she won't be able to make it to the barn hall dance."

"Now *that's* a shame. I was hoping you two would..."

He arched a brow. "Would do what, Ma?"

"Oh, nothing."

"Ma, what have you been up to?"

He folded his arms across his chest.

"Oh, nothing son. It's just that your brothers have gotten lucky under that old mistletoe in the barn. You know kissing under the mistletoe brings good luck to the couple under it."

He grinned and shook his head. I think that time has passed for me, Ma. I've had my chance with a family."

"Now, son. Don't give up on love. You know as I said to your brothers, the man upstairs will give you beauty for ashes. All you need to do is have a little faith and a little hope. Even faith as small as a mustard seed. Nothing can ever replace your beautiful family; may they rest in heavenly peace. But they would want you to be happy. There's such a thing as second chances."

Cameron would love to believe so. He could have tried harder to get Cat to stay but he didn't want to risk being hurt again. But maybe his mother was right. His brothers had taken a chance on finding love again and it worked out for them. The problem was, would it work out for Cameron too? Or was he destined to remain single for the rest of his life. Cat probably wanted to move on and find some city guy to spend the rest of her life with.

Her life was in New York now, not in the small town of Mistletoe. She said it herself; she might be from the small town but she identified as a city girl. Would she even be happy there with him? His life was the ranch, his family, the Mistletoe church and the children's center. He didn't have room in his life for anything else. Or anyone else. Or was it because he was afraid to make room for anyone else?

Chapter 13

The Annual Charming Ranch Christmas Barn Hall Dance was upon them.

It seemed as if everyone in the town of Mistletoe made it to the celebration. The barn hall was decorated in bright festive lights and garlands around. Music from the speakers played. Earlier that day, they spent the morning in Church after breakfast.

Luncheon was served at the homeless shelter in town. Then it was the dinner. And now the dance.

The Charming family liked to keep up the tradition that had been in the family for over a hundred years.

It was Christmas. And although he felt happy for the guests filing into the barn, there was something missing inside him.

There was something missing from his life.

Cat.

He'd only just became reacquainted with her this month, yet she made a deep impression on him. It was as if they'd always been together all these years without missing a beat. It was as if they'd never been apart.

The re-connection felt so real.

Was this really a second chance?

Well, if it was, it looked as if his second chance had flown back to New York.

They'd spent the last few weeks, sharing so much joy. Playing Mr. and Mrs. Santa Clause for the kids at the hospital. Sharing laughter and stories. How could he gave gotten it all wrong?

How could it have ended so soon?

Should he have asked her to stay?

But that wouldn't be fair to her, would it?

She had a life outside of him. And that life was calling to her. It wanted her back.

"You look gloomy, bro," his brother Carter said, as a lively version of O Holy Night played over the speakers. "Where's Cat?"

Cat had a chance to spend time with Cameron's family when she'd finished the draft of her book. They all loved her—as they always had. She really made an impression on them this month, especially his mother who told him it was so good to see him smile again.

"She's on a flight to New York," Cameron said, his heart aching at those words.

"New York?"

"Yes, she's turning in her manuscript and then working on her blog. She has a lot of sponsors she has to please."

"Looks like you're not one of them."

"Nope."

"Hey, man, I'm really sorry about that. You two looked so happy these past few weeks."

A knot tightened in his stomach. Yes, he had been happy, but just as with his late wife and child, it was as if happiness wasn't meant to last around him.

He tried to push the negative thought out of his head, his heart, but it wasn't easy.

Carter then turned back to Cameron and said, "Bro, how's your eyesight?"

His brother and he always played around and teased each other.

"It's fine, why?"

"Oh, nothing. It's just that you said Cat was on a flight to New York. You sure about that now?" Carter arched a brow.

When Cameron turned around, his heart leaped inside his chest.

"Cat?" he said as she walked into the Barn Hall.

She looked breathtaking.

She wore her hair down and had the most beautiful satin red festive dress that seemed to hug her curves. Her lipstick matched her dress, the rouge was like a delicious shade of strawberry.

Was this real?

Was he imagining this?

"Hey, cowboy," she said to him when they were inches apart.

"Hey, Cat. You look amazing! Beautiful."

Her cheeks colored.

"Thank you. So do you. I mean you look handsome."

"Thanks. I thought you were in New York?"

"I had a change of plans."

"You did."

"Well, I had a change of heart. I had so much fun here and I decided to extend my rent on the cabin. I want to stay here in Mistletoe."

"But what about your grandfather?"

"He asked me about my time here, and I told him. He told me he was having fun at the retirement center and told me he'd see me in the New Year. He insisted I stay here. He's still not into celebrating Christmas right now. But I have a feeling I'm going to change his mind soon."

A warm feeling came over Cameron.

"I think he'd be happy to see you happy."

She chuckled. "I was afraid," she said to him.

"Afraid of what?"

"Of taking a chance on being with someone again after you know who."

He grinned.

"And now?" he asked, reassuringly.

"And now, I'm thinking why would I paint my future with the colors of the past? The past is gone. You and I have known each other since high school. You're such a good guy, Cameron. I love the way I feel when I'm with you."

"I love the way I feel when I'm with you too. I know it's hard. Trust me. But as Ma says, sometimes we've just got to put our trust in doing the right thing. Knowing that He'll always look out for us."

"Amen to that."

"Would you like to dance?" he asked.

"I'd love to."

They moved onto the dance floor and danced, touching her skin while holding her hand gave him a light feeling.

After the dance, she looked up.

"Is that the famous mistletoe?" she asked.

"You've heard about it then," he said, unable to hide his grin.

"Everyone has. The legend is that whoever kisses under it will have good luck and a happy relationship."

"It actually worked out well for two of my brothers. You see them over there?" Cameron pointed out.

"Wow, you mean their wives met them here?"

"Well, sort of."

She leaned closer to him.

A smile curved the corners of his lips.

"Well, cowboy," she said. "How about it?"

He leaned closer to her and they kissed under the mistletoe, her lips were as soft as they looked. The kiss was magical. Delight shivered through him.

She's the one.

That thought just slid through him. He never thought he could be happy again but right now he wanted to make Cat as happy as he felt right now.

They sealed their future with the mistletoe kiss just as his brothers had done. And he looked forward to spending more time with Cat and a future filled with hope and happiness.

COWBOY'S CHRISTMAS WISH

By J. A. Somers

COWBOY'S CHRISTMAS WISH

Cole Charming is one cowboy who is never going to fall in love—again. The cowboy-turned-actor had a very public breakup that shattered his heart. After going back to his hometown during the holidays, he bumps into Katie, a sweet girl he had a crush on from high school. When sparks fly between them he knows he needs to keep his distance. He wouldn't want to ruin a good friendship.

Katie finds herself in a sticky place. She's the last in her family to get married and as a wedding event planner, that doesn't help her brand. Now, at her grandparents' anniversary, the heat is on. The last thing she wanted to do was to stand out as the only one without a date. In walks her high school crush. The tall, dark and handsome Cole Charming. The pity-looks from everyone at the event were more than she could handle. Will this handsome cowboy step in to save her face?

"Love is patient, love is kind."
– 1 Corinthians 13:4-5

Chapter 1

"So what do you wish for, cowboy?" Cole Charming's brother Evan placed his hand on Cole's shoulder as he overlooked the tall Christmas Wishing Tree in the barn hall.

The festive decorations illuminated the cozy rustic barn hall.

An upbeat tempo of the holiday hymn *Joy to the World* blared through the speakers. The mood was electric. Hopeful.

He wished he could start all over again. *That's* what he wished for.

This cowboy did not feel he deserved a second chance at happiness. He'd messed up in his relationships in the past. Sure, he loved women and he loved to flirt. That was his style. He just never got too close to any of them. As soon as things got serious, he'd distanced himself as he always did, and that drove his exes into the arms of another man.

He was beginning to wonder what was going on in his head.

He was a ladies' man who dated a lot in the past but never liked to commit to a serious relationship. He was out of there like a house on fire.

He'd been abandoned as a child and ended up in foster care until the Charmings took him in and adopted him. He was thankful to be a part of a caring family but he still had issues when it came to commitment. Serious issues.

Guests already started to file into the place. The Charmings held their annual Christmas barn dance every year. But this year, they were also hosting an anniversary dinner. They didn't always rent out the barn hall, but this time was different.

The Christmas Wishing Tree had significance. It was where a young woman during the second world war came to wish that her beau would be home safely and for the war to end. Her wishes came true and they got married right here in the barn 75 years ago. What a love story. Well, at least his grandparents and parents thought so. They wanted the couple to relive that moment and have their dinner there.

Cole thought since the latest episode of his TV show wrapped up filming in Hollywood until after the holidays, he'd return back home to Mistletoe, to spend Christmas with his family and friends. Especially, his good friend Mike who was organizing the event with his sister, Katie.

Just then he felt a sweet sensation slide inside him thinking about Katie.

"Nothing," Cole replied to his brother. "I don't wish for anything right now. What's the point?"

"Oh, come on now. Where's the holiday spirit? It's two weeks to Christmas. And today's the anniversary dance."

"Yeah." The lights on the tree flickered with the rhythm of the holiday music playing. He could see the lovely decorations glistening. But he felt anything but joyful right now. Last year, he'd broken up with one of his co-stars on his hit TV show. He felt as empty as his cup of eggnog right now.

Let's face it, relationships weren't easy. And his public break-up almost ruined his reputation. The break up was ugly and sensational. He was glad to be back in his hometown, away from the paparazzi and the drama.

He'd prayed to the man upstairs to give him a sign, to let him know what to do. He didn't tell anyone, not any of his eight brothers, but he was still torn up inside over his breakup. He was a cowboy. And he was someone that always excelled at amusing people. He was always good at hiding his feelings and playing someone else—that's what drew him to acting. Maybe that's why he couldn't or wouldn't get too close to anyone. He didn't want to show his true self.

His ex left him for their other co-star. Talk about tension on the set. He was half hoping the writers on his show would write him off. Just as his ex had done.

Right now, he preferred to be out here with the wide-open spaces, the horses and the animals. Especially with his mom and his brothers and cousins.

"Darling, when did you get back in town?" his adoptive mother Lucinda walked over with garlands over her forearm, she was helping out with the last-minute touches. The barn hall looked like a magical winter wonderland.

She reached up and he reached down to hug her. He hadn't seen his mother in too long. He loved that woman more than anything on earth.

"Not too long ago. Thought I'd make myself useful around here." He paused. "Good to see you again, Ma."

"Good to see you too." She beamed.

"Mike told me his grandparents' anniversary dinner is being held here later."

"Yes, I hope you can stay," she said, hopefully.

He thought about that for a moment.

Butterflies exploded in his stomach. He knew who would be here tonight too. Katie. His secret crush from high school.

Mike's little sister. And that knocked him sideways. Not only was dating a sister of a friend totally off limits, but Cole and his brothers had sworn to live the bachelor life.

His mother wanted to see them all happy, she knew that when they were in relationships, they were happy as bunnies. But she just wanted to see them settle down before she went to be with the Lord one day, with their dad.

His mother and her sister Aunt Nellie were also the matchmakers of the church. They felt bad that the Charming brothers were hard to match up with anyone in town.

Did he want to stay in town? Should he? He said he'd help run some errands for Mike later. But there's one person he didn't know if he should see.

And that was Katie.

Chapter 2

Later, Katie Smyth rummaged through her dinner purse one more time looking for her Santa-themed ID badge and key card. It was a few weeks to Christmas and the holiday music boomed over the sound speakers. Sleigh Ride played. She was the event planner, and she should have an ID to prove it. More guests were filing into the Barn.

Please, Lord. Let me not be embarrassed tonight. I want the night to go perfect for my grandparents.

Oh, and please no *family politics tonight. Please.*

She'd organized her grandparents 75th anniversary and now the day had finally come. They had gotten married near Christmas just after the second world war ended when her grandfather came back from serving overseas.

They married at the Charming Ranch so long ago and wanted to come back full circle to the same place with all their children and grand-children and great-grandchildren to celebrate with them. Of course, the barn looked a lot different then. It was newly-renovated and converted into a rustic luxury event hall.

Unfortunately, she was the only Smyth in her family who hadn't provided them with great-grandchildren.

That was something Kate had always wanted. To get married and to have children. But it didn't look like it was going to happen any time soon. Not while she was in her mid-thirties and no prospects in sight. Her sisters and her one brother, Mike, were all happily married.

Her own engagement was broken off and she'd given up on love after that.

Still, she was always the go-to-organizer for anything. While growing up she'd organized her dolls, her books, her friend's clothes. And later as she got older, she would organize the ornaments in the house, and her baking spices and comfort foods in the cabinets—her waistline showed evidence of her other hobby, food.

She was what some would call curvy. Food had become her comfort. Her food hobby started when she was teased in high school. Then again after Pete, her ex, left her for a super thin model—her own cousin Roxie! Imagine that.

People in small towns talk. Everybody knew everybody's business, so that didn't help her pride to heal any sooner. Nor the gossip about her being single at her age. It didn't help that all her siblings and cousins, including now Roxie, were happily married.

She'd tried the church single's ministry, but that didn't help. She didn't connect with anyone there.

She had begun to think something was wrong with her, until she found the perfect course in college and started her own business. She was good at organizing events and making others happy so she became a wedding planner.

She figured, if she couldn't have her own wedding then why not make it happen for others? In a grand way.

Just then, a sweet chill came over her. She stopped and looked up. It was as if instinct was alerting her to a presence. Then she saw him across the barn hall and her heart stopped.

Stop drooling, Katie.

It was him.

Her brother's friend from high school.

Cole Charming.

Cole was a sweet and charming yet troubled cowboy who used to get into a little trouble at school. He got expelled once for fighting. It was over her. Someone had pushed her down off her bike. And he was nearby and saw what happened and then went after the guy. She was eternally grateful for that.

He was her mad crush from high school—even before that incident, but he was also her brother's best friend and well, seeing him was just so out of the question.

He worked on his parents' ranch until heading west after he was discovered by a talent scout. He now co-starred in the TV series *Random*.

What on earth was Cole Charming doing at her grandparents' anniversary celebration?

"Smile for the camera," Louis, the part time videographer and the town's on-call gossip said to Katie as he made the rounds around the crowded barn hall.

Previously he'd been asking everyone to say a message into the camera and then pretended to interview them. Thankfully, he hadn't asked her anything just yet, except where was her date earlier and that was thankfully off camera, because she had no date tonight.

Katie gave a quick smile and a wave.

"Thanks, Katie," Louis said with a wink. "We're just capturing every minute for the wedding anniversary album and for your grandparents' anniversary party. What time will they be here?"

"Soon. They're not expecting this elaborate celebration. It will be quite a surprise." She beamed inside thinking of how much they'd been through, how much they'd help build the family, and how much they so deserved this.

"Nice celebration, cuz. You really outdid yourself this time." Her cousin Lucy nodged Katie with a glass of eggnog in her hand.

The holiday music had already started playing so everyone was on the barn's dance floor now. Well, almost everyone. It was a nice environment, rustic, yet elegant. One would never know they were inside a barn, unless they looked up at the intricate designs to see the structure. The floor had been renovated already. The beautiful red Poinsettias plants adorned each table. She was glad the Charming's rented out the wedding venue when her grandparents requested it so close to Christmas. They wanted to be here, but they just don't know how elaborate the celebration would be—and how many out-of-towners came to make the occasion.

"Thanks. I'm glad everyone's having a good time," Katie said.

"That's Cole Charming, isn't it?" Lucy added, pointing her glass over to the far corner.

"Yes," Katie said, hoping her cousin would not see the rouge in her cheeks.

"Where's your ID badge?" Lucy asked.

"It must have fallen off somewhere."

Katie had been helping Mrs. Fletcher, from the church, get seated when it slipped off. Mrs. Fletcher was in her nineties and fit as a fiddle save for her knee replacement which acted up at times.

Katie loved that the senior members of the church including her own grandparents, were active in the community.

They had so much wisdom and spunk. It was true about the third act in life, the sixties to nineties range. So much to give, so much energy, so many renewals and it's even more special when you get to share it with the one you love.

Still, Katie had to find her badge soon. Her brother had insisted on everyone wearing their name tag so their grandparents and everyone knew who was who.

Earlier she had gone back to the table but her badge wasn't there. She was probably going to get kicked out of her own event. Everyone had to wear one. That was the rule. It wasn't a royal wedding reception or anything—but it might as well have been.

Her brother Mike had insisted on it. He was a high-profile cowboy businessman who didn't take chances with security, even in a small town like Mistletoe. He didn't want any party crashers. This event had to be perfect celebration for Grandma and Grandpa.

***

Cole's eyes captured Katie's beauty across the barn hall, surreptitiously, while he was helping to set up the extra sound speaker in the far corner. His gaze drifted to her as she worked the room making sure last-minute touches and Christmas wedding decorations were in pristine condition. She moved so gracefully like a swan. She always had that classy way about her.

If he wasn't mistaken, he thought he caught her glimpsing in his direction a couple times.

Too bad the one he had his eyes one was the one he could never have.

Mike then stepped back inside the barn.

"You need help, bro," Mike said.

"I'm almost done here," Cole said.

Bro?

Why did Mike call him bro just now?

Oh, great. Just another reminder that it could never or would never work out, even if he asked Katie for a date. Which he would never do. Ever. It meant too much for him to keep his friendship with Mike—who was like a brother to him. They'd been through so much together growing up in Mistletoe. Even though Cole moved out west to California, he still visited his small hometown and he and Mike had a secret business on the side too. They weren't going to tell anyone about it, until it fully up and running.

"You looked like you were in a daze a moment ago. Something on your mind?" Mike asked casually.

They'd both finished up with the speaker. The sound coming through was crystal clear and sweet. Holiday music really got the Christmas vibe going.

"Nothing's on my mind."

"You sure?" Mike asked, clearly not convinced.

No.

"Yes, I'm sure."

"Hey, man. I'm really sorry about you and..."

"It's okay. I'm just glad she's happy now. I think this whole marriage business is just not for me."

"Hey don't say that. And don't let your mother hear you say that." Mike teased him, but Mike knew how persistent Cole's mother could be in wanting to see her boys happy and happily married.

Cole just felt marriage wasn't for him.

The only one he thought about he couldn't have anyway. So what was the point? He would just be a lifelong bachelor like his uncle Ted back in Wyoming. His uncle was estranged from his family and moved out of Mistletoe years ago. He hadn't heard from him since but he hoped he was all right.

"You know you can tell me anything, right?" Mike persisted.

"I know."

"Good. My ears are always open."

"You sure about that? I thought it was your mouth," Cole teased his friend. They always did this banter back and forth between them.

Mike was really there for him back in the day. And vice-versa. They used to stick up for each other all the time.

That's why guilt swept through him that he had some feelings for Mike's younger sister but couldn't let Mike know about it. It would kill their friendship, and it would probably kill *him* too.

"Listen, I have to head back out, cowboy," Mike said. "And thanks again for the help."

"Hey, no problem man. Anytime."

***

Katie's gaze slid again to Cole, the cowboy who had a reputation of being a ladies' man. The man stood at over six feet tall, with broad shoulders and lean thighs. He looked sweet in his cowboy hat and suit. Was he single? He'd had so many supermodels on his arms during the past few years, it was hard to keep up. Well, that's what she found out previously during a Google search to find out how he was doing.

Oh, why was she glancing at Cole. He was off limits. Her brother's best friend. And she had to focus on the anniversary event.

She was glad he came to support her family.

And speaking of which...

"Isn't it nice that everyone is having such a good time. This reminds of the Hollywood private weddings. Mom and Dad will be happy when they arrive," Aunt Jackie said with a glass of eggnog in her hand. She was always on her social media page about which celebrity was getting married. It seemed as if wedding bells were always in the air.

Hollywood private weddings?

Aunt Jackie loved talking about the rich and famous.

Katie was so not like that. She felt as if she didn't fit in sometimes. Didn't matter what a person did for a living or had in the bank accounts. It's what was in their hearts that counted. At least in her books.

The festive energy in the barn hall was amazing, the atmosphere was electric with the sounds of people laughing and chatting amongst each other. She loved weddings and gatherings—well sometimes.

She loved seeing her family gather.

Everyone said her grandmother reminded them of Betty White, so youthful and vibrant in her golden years.

A wave of joy rushed through Katie as she envisioned their expressions when her grandparents eventually arrive. Would she ever find someone to grow old with like her grandparents?

To share her life and dreams and love with? To raise a family with?

She was so proud of Nana. Her grandmother was listed in some record book as being the oldest resident in the town to participate in a marathon at age 85. Grandma was now 95 and still looking fit. She'd shown Katie her sequenced dress earlier.

Katie hoped she would look that good when she got to that age. Grandma was a fun spirit who always encouraged her grandchildren and always took them to church when they were little. She was fit as a fiddle and always had a scripture ready when she gave them encouragement during their difficult times.

"Love makes life beautiful," she'd once told Katie and her cousins. Bless her soul. Her grandma met Grandpa when she was a teenager and it had been love at first sight and happily ever after.

She'd told her grandchildren it was her dream to see her grandchildren settle down and get married before she goes to be with the Lord.

So out of her ten grandchildren, all were married. Except Katie. Though she came close before.

Her ex had never missed a chance to tell Katie she'd look so much better if she'd lose weight. Like a lot. She never did fit in with his circle. Of course, he didn't mind having her around to help him with his college work.

Aunt Jackie kept slipping in remarks about if only she'd lose weight her ex might have stayed with her, or if only she'd made herself more attractive by losing a bit of weight.

Katie got used to gently sweeping those comments out of her mind.

Her grandma always told her the Lord could make a way where there was none. Everything happened in its time.

Right now, her focus was on making beautiful weddings for others. Her heart still needed a bit of healing after her ex-fiancé left her. Focusing on others was a good way to get out of that rut.

Her grandparents stuck together like white on rice. And speaking of rice.

She spoke into the mouthpiece wrapped around her head to talk to her assistant at the other end of the barn.

"All set?"

"Yes, ma'am." He always called her ma'am.

"Great. And please, call me Katie."

She knew they wanted rice tossed at the bride and groom as per their family tradition.

Her family still insisted on it. It was supposed to symbolize rain, which is said to be a sign of prosperity, fertility and good fortune. Um, well maybe fertility was something her grandparents no longer needed.

Everything at the reception was on cue. She held her earpiece close.

"Dave, do you have the rice?" Her grandparents wanted to re-enact their special day with their grandchildren.

"Sure thing, Katie. All on cue."

"And the song, *I'll be Home for Christmas*?"

"It's all ready."

A warm smile curved her lips. At least something was going right. When her grandfather served in the armed forces, he wasn't sure he'd see her grandmother again, so he always sang that song and wrote a letter quoting the lyrics. The last part was sad because some of the soldiers didn't know if they would be home for Christmas. But then the war ended in September and many of them were home for Christmas. Grandpa didn't want to waste any time in marrying his sweetheart.

The warm story of love and commitment melted her heart every time.

Later, Katie walked around to make sure everything was in place. After all, her grandparents didn't want to stay up too late after they arrived. They had church in the morning. And the younger crowd would still hang around and listen to the festive music, enjoying the decorations and engaging in talk way into the night.

"Oh, my goodness. I'm going over there to talk to him," a woman near her table whispered. "He's so hot. I can't believe he's here," another woman beside the first woman whispered.

She turned to see who they were talking about and yep, it was Cole, all right.

"Wait, he's coming this way," another woman said.

Katie could not believe how much they were ogling over Cole. Well, actually, she could believe it. He was breathtaking.

But he was an actor and she didn't want to date another actor. She might have had a crush on him back in high school but that was then. This was now.

When she realized they were telling the truth. Her belly exploded into butterflies. What was she doing?

Why was her body reacting to him like that?

The closer he came, the more she tingled inside.

She'd never felt that way about any man before, not since high school. Not even with Pete, her ex.

Just then, he was walking over towards her, a glass of eggnog in his hand.

A gorgeous grin on his face. If her brother caught her even talking with his best friend, he would not like it at all.

Her brother was ever so protective of his sisters. All of them. And she was no exception.

She never told her brother about her crush on his friend.

What would he do now if he found out she liked his best friend? A cowboy with a history of being a ladies' man—and one that always changed dates.

Before he could make it across the barn to her, a group of women closed in around him.

Chapter 3

Waves of excitement rolled through Cole Charming as the sound *Holly Jolly Christmas* sounded over the speakers in the barn. That's how he felt, eyeing the lovely brunette event planner across the barn.

But before he could walk across the barn to see sweet Katie, a group of women circled around him.

"You're Cole Charming," one of them said. "Can I have your autograph?"

He was speechless. He wasn't expecting this. Of course, he always appreciated his fans, but he didn't expect to be swarmed by them at the Anniversary dance tonight.

Oh boy.

"Hey, you all right here?" Mike said, slapping his back, noticing he needed rescuing from the group of fans.

"No problem. You need some more help?"

"Sure. Sorry, ladies, I need to steal Cole for a minute."

The women looked disappointed but one blew him a kiss and told him she'd see him later. Cole felt bad for them, but he was beginning to think he should have worn a disguise. He really didn't want anyone to recognize him tonight. Besides, he was also a changed cowboy. There was a time when he loved to flirt, but not now. And he didn't want any attention on him. It was an anniversary dinner for a golden couple. They should be the spotlight tonight, not him.

He prayed Mike didn't see him looking at his sister earlier. That was a big mistake. What was he doing? He knew Mike was overly protective of the women in his family, and he couldn't blame him one bit.

"Have you seen Katie yet?" Mike asked when they got to a corner alone.

Cole stopped breathing for a second. Guilt slid through him. "Uh, I think she's busy."

"Go and say hi. I'm sure she'll appreciate it. You did a great job getting us this venue for the anniversary dance."

Cole felt heat climb inside him. "Hey, it's nothing. We're practically family."

Yeah, family. And families don't date—each other.

"Listen, man," Mike said. "I've got to go back to the party store to pick up some more balloons."

"Want a ride?"

"I'm good. See you later."

With those words, Cole sucked in a deep breath and took Mike's advice to speak to Katie. Guilt shadowed every step he took across the barn hall. She was a stunning vision of loveliness. He had to see Katie but keep it all professional.

That was going to be hard.

Chapter 4

The cowboy standing before Katie made her weak in the knees.

Cole Charming.

Her eyes gazed into his soft blue eyes, the color of the ocean on a cloudless summer day, she was drowning in the blueness of them.

His shapely lips were swoon worthy. What would those lovely lips feel like against hers? She had to pull herself together. He was so off limits. Her brother's best friend. Not gonna happen anytime soon.

She drew in a deep breath, trying to get her bearings as her heart fluttered in her chest. She must focus. She must not hold her breath. He was just a handsome cowboy turned actor.

Yet, as calm as she might have appeared on the outside, he made her shiver with delight inside, and he had no idea how much.

"Katie, it's so good to see you again," he said in a low sensual voice, so silky and deep, she felt as if she was going to swoon over him uncontrollably.

"Cole," she said, her lips trembling slightly as she took him in with her eyes. "It's good to see you too."

She could not believe how stunning he looked today. He was always breathtaking. But now? She couldn't tear her gaze away from him.

Then, she just remembered, she was in control. Of the event, not her feelings or her thoughts about Cole. But at least she was in control of something tonight.

"You're doing an amazing job here tonight," he said.

"Thank you." Her tongue was tied. That was all she could muster right now.

The tall handsome cowboy was impeccably dressed in some nice dark grey suit. His shoulders were broad and fine. His facial features so model-like with his chiselled cheekbones that looked like they could dodge a bullet. His smooth dark-tanned complexion was eye-candy.

He was everything on her checklist, except, he was not someone she should date.

He was also an actor, like her ex. A big no-no.

"You look amazing," he said.

"So do you. It's really good to see you again," she said, breathing hard, aware that his eyes were penetrating hers. A slight grin of amusement curled the corners of his sweet shapely lips when she fumbled for words. Why was she nervous around him?

She was confident all evening. But now?

Like seriously?

This was so not like her.

There seemed to be a spark in his eyes. Or was that her imagination? His eyes were another thing.

She was too afraid to look deep into his eyes again for fear she'd never get out of that trans he'd almost put her into when he walked up to her.

"I'm glad you came out to support my grandparents."

"Wouldn't miss it for the world. Your folks are good people."

"Thank you. I guess our families go way back."

That was the problem, their families were so close, almost like—family.

She caught a few more women ogling him from the corner of her eye. But he was speaking to her, wasn't he?

"You dropped this," the handsome cowboy said, eyeing her beautifully.

She glanced down and saw her ID badge.

Relief washed over her. She let out a deep breath she didn't realize she was holding.

He had her ID with her name and her photo and access card—something she didn't want to ever lose again.

"You found my badge! I was looking for that earlier," she said. "Thank you so much!" And she really meant it.

"I figured you might need it. You have to be careful with key cards. In the wrong hands they could easily get reprogrammed by hacks."

That's exactly what she was afraid of. She'd lived in the big city before and worked in an IT department too. A lot of crazy stuff could happen in the wrong hands.

But thank the Lord, her ID and credentials ended up in the right hands.

Like the prince and the glass slipper, right?

Stop that line of wishful thinking, Katie. There's no such thing as fairy tales. This was just a coincidence. Nothing more.

Cole handed Katie her ID badge and his soft fingers brushed her hand, her tummy tickled inside. Electricity pulsed through her blood.

She'd never touched his hand before.

"I..." *Can't think....can't breathe in front of him.* "I'm really thankful you found it," she said.

Her ID case included her driver's licence and credit card along with her house key in the laminated ID pouch behind her photo ID credential.

My goodness. What if it had fallen into the wrong hands?

But it didn't. It fell into the right hands. And what beautiful soft hands they were.

She glanced around to see if her brother was anywhere. Not that it mattered. She was only speaking to Cole. He was a guest. And soon, the party would begin. Her grandparents should be there soon.

Just then, her jaw fell open in horror when in walked her ex Pete with her cousin Roxie, holding hands.

Chapter 5

Oh, no. Not this. Not now.

Panic swept through Katie.

What were they doing here? She didn't think they'd actually come. The night was turning out to be a disaster and the guests of honor, her grandparents, weren't even there yet.

"Well, look who showed up," Aunt Jackie said, walking over to Katie. "Your ex and Roxie. The nerve of them to show up here. You okay, Katie?" she said, a pitiful look on her face.

That was the last thing Katie needed was the looks of pity on everyone's faces. The last time Pete was around the family was when they announced their engagement at a family picnic.

Now, he was there with her cousin Roxie.

Roxie wore a white sequenced gown.

"Who would wear white to someone else's wedding reunion reception?" Aunt Jackie added.

"A person who would date her cousin's ex-fiance," her cousin Lucy added. Lucy just approached them when she saw the commotion.

"Is that a little bump in her belly?" another guest asked out loud.

Everyone seemed to gather around the couple and nod their approval. Pete was doing well with rave reviews on his new play and Roxie was doing some TV drama and had a busy social media page. And now they were pregnant?

Katie just wished she could leave right now. But she wouldn't. It's her grandparents' anniversary dinner and dance, and she was the event planner.

The turns and stares and back-and-forth looks directed at Pete, Roxie and Katie was just too much to bear, followed by looks of pity for Katie.

"Oh, this doesn't look good at all," Aunt Jackie said. "You shouldn't have shown up alone. You're the only one who doesn't have a date and your ex is..."

"It's all right, Auntie."

Could Katie feel any lower?

What happened to the holiday spirit?

Her spirit was anywhere but up, right now.

Everyone was supposed to be looking jovial anticipating her grandparents' arrival. Now? They had looks of pity and the tension was so thick in the air, you could cut it with a steak knife.

Oh, Lord please don't let there be any more tension here. Please let this evening go all right, according to plan.

She took a swig of eggnog wanting to finish the entire glass then down another, but she chose not to.

She would not drown her sorrows in rich-tasting delicious eggnog tonight.

And she was not going to be the guest of honor at her own pity party, either.

She was the organizer and she would make sure the arrangements and decorations were in pristine condition. Then she would check on the rice confetti.

Katie excused herself from Cole, her aunt and her cousin telling them she had to check on something.

She placed her glass on the table and made her way to the other side of the banquet hall to check on the decorations when her dress got caught on a chair and tore.

The music had quieted down and it was as if the rip was audible for everyone to hear in the barn hall.

Everyone froze. All pairs of embarrassed eyes were on Katie.

Chapter 6

A wave of disappointment rushed through Cole when he heard the chatter and giggles directed at sweet Katie. A surge of urgency to protect her came over him.

Cole couldn't let Katie go through this alone.

He didn't like the looks she was getting. It bothered him. He saw and heard what was going on?

Could they make her feel any worse?

He wanted to jump in and say something.

Katie looked embarrassed and said nothing for a moment. He could see a hint of rouge coloring her cheeks.

She always did that in high school whenever she was put in a corner. He remembered that a long time ago when the teacher would pick on her in class and ask her an awkward question. Or the high school bully pointed out her weight.

He heard whispers about the mystery couple stealing the show. It was her cousin Roxie and her ex-fiancé Pete.

Cole made his way over to Katie who managed to free herself.

"Are you all right?" he asked gently.

"Yes, I'm good." Her words said one thing but those pretty little cheeks of hers said another. If they were any redder, they could pass for strawberries on her cheeks.

"Darling, are you okay?" the editor for the *Mistletoe News* was there and gave Katie and pitying look.

"I'm good. My dress just got a little caught."

"Oh, no, you don't look too well," a man with a woman on his arm said to her.

"Maybe I shouldn't have come," Pete said to Katie as he walked over to her. "I can see you still feel bad about...well, my engagement to Roxie."

"Bad?" She gave a nervous chuckle. "Why would I feel bad?" Her voice was an octave higher than normal.

"Katie, I hope you can see that Pete and I love each other," Roxie said, stepping towards her. "I hope you can move on."

The crowd gathered around and Katie looked mortified.

"I have moved on," Katie responded.

"I know you'll find someone soon," Roxie said.

"She has," Cole heard himself say.

What was he doing?

"I have?" she whispered to him turning to his side so that no one else could hear her.

"Katie and I are serious," Cole said. "And we're both happy for you."

Cole had done many things in his time and dated many women, but he'd never go out with a relative of his ex, much less marry them then show up to a family gathering. Seemed like Katie deserved much better than what her cousin and her ex were doing.

He wished right now he could reach out and make it all better for her. Just as she'd done in high school whenever he was having trouble with the subject he hated in high school. He aced most of his subjects. But he could never take history because of the way the teacher taught it. Made it sound monotone. Yet, she'd always been there as his study pal and made up some poems to make it easy to remember stuff. What a gal.

Right now, Cole had no idea what got into him. If there was one thing he couldn't stand, it was public shaming.

There was nothing wrong with being single, but rubbing it in someone's face was just not cool in his books. He wanted to shut their mouths once and for all. He was an actor but he was still a cowboy.

And this was a role that was needed. He could tell by the look of embarrassment on Katie's face. He knew what she was feeling when she got that way.

"You okay, darling? Can I get you more eggnog?" he asked, rubbing her arm gently.

He immediately saw her body relax. She looked relieved and mouthed, *thank you*. "Sure, darling, I'd love that," she added in a more confident voice.

The other women's jaws fell wide open. Her ex and her cousin both looked equally as stunned.

Then her brother Mike came by.

"You and Cole are seeing each other?" The look of shock flashed across Mike's face. "When were you going to tell me this?"

Chapter 7

Oh, no. Things are about to get worse.

The two cowboys stood facing each other. A menacing look on her brother Mike's face. This was not good.

Katie saw Cole pull Mike aside and talk to him in a low voice as the holiday music began to sound again over the speakers.

A guest pulled her aside to help out with one of the decorations that had fallen. She immediately went to sort that out. All the while praying the boys wouldn't do anything silly. Not today of all days.

Later when she returned, hoping there wouldn't be a fight she'd have to break up, she was pleasantly surprised to see the men having a good chuckle.

"Oh, I get it." Mike seemed a bit more relieved.

"It's okay, sis," Mike then came over to Katie. "I totally understand." He then patted Cole on the back and made his way through the crowd mingling with the guests.

Well, disaster averted. Again. Thank you, Lord.

"What did you say to Mike? He's calm as a gingerbread man," Katie said.

Cole smiled and a cute dimple surfaced on his left cheek.

"I told him it's only pretense to get your ex to cool it."

Her heart fluttered in her chest, but then a sinking feeling slid through her.

It's only pretense.

Well, duh. Of course it is. It's the Christmas season, your grandparents' reunion. You're the only one without a date. And your ex and your cousin showed up together.

She sucked in a deep breath.

She was truly thankful for what Cole did just now. He was a true cowboy with all heart. But why did she feel sorry that after tonight, it would be all over.

It would all be gone. The magic, the moment, the feeling, the time with him.

It was only pretense.

She couldn't get the disappointment out of her mind.

A wave of heartwarming heat rushed through her. She could not believe this was happening.

Did Cole Charming seriously just rescue her out of that embarrassing situation?

She would be eternally grateful, even though she was okay with being single. Well, actually, the truth was, deep down, she wished she'd found that special one. She really wanted to be as happy with a soulmate as her grandparents.

Okay, she sure didn't want her ex to think she hadn't moved on or for anyone to keep throwing pity looks her way. That was so not cool.

She would never be able to repay Cole for rescuing her from Public Humiliation 101—according to the Smyth family.

Everything was being captured on video. Could you imagine years from now how everyone would be talking about the pitiful single thirty-something who's ex moved on while she remained the last to get married in her family circle—if at all?

Not that she was about keeping up appearances but the truth was she needed that friendly support from her old high school crush.

Okay, maybe burying herself in her work to avoid getting her heart burned again wasn't exactly the best strategy.

Oh, why didn't she show up with a date?

The truth was, she thought she didn't need to prove anything. Well, she didn't exactly feel that great now, did she? Not in front of all her family and family friends.

She never thought she'd feel such feelings towards her cowboy in shining armor for the occasion either. She was stunned to feel the rekindled feelings she'd had for him back in high school.

My, how things have changed, not.

Well, he was an actor. And he was a very good one, too.

"You two are an item?" one of the guests asked incredulously.

As if she couldn't land a hot Hollywood actor like Cole Charming. Okay, maybe she couldn't, but they didn't have to know *that*, did they?

"Sure, I didn't want to say at the time. Today's about Grandma and Grandad."

What was she doing? Why was she lying to keep up appearances? This was so not like her. Did it matter? What if they found it was all a big fat lie?

In a small town, gossip travels faster than email.

Cole had taken a glass of eggnog off a tray from one of the waiters making the rounds and handed it to his darling love—well, that's the way he made it look the way his magnetic charm worked as he captured her with his beautiful eyes.

"Thank you, darling," she said.

"No problem, beautiful."

"Um, why didn't you tell me you were dating Cole Charming?" her aunt Jackie said, walking over to her, still in shock, as if she didn't remember that Cole was standing right there.

"Well, I didn't want to say anything at the time. You know I like to keep my life private." Well, sort of anyway.

A charming grin of amusement touched the corner of Cole's sweet sexy lips and at that instant, she really wished it was true. She wished it wasn't just a staged-romance to save face act.

Man, he was gorgeous. Too stunning for his own good. For *her* own good. She could not resist him. He'd always had that effect on her, but she could not believe that the feeling for him had intensified over the years. She'd never felt this way with Pete.

It was as if she and Cole had this magical chemistry between them, an electric pulse between them that lingered in the air.

The sweet intoxicating scent of his aftershave wafted to her nostrils and delighted her. She could tell he worked out at the gym.

He was delicious and charming.

Oh, why couldn't this be the real thing?

When the reception ended later tonight, so would their charade and it tore a hole in her heart as wide as the Mistletoe River.

Chapter 8

Later that night, Grandma and Grandad came into the barn hall to cheers from everyone. Her grandmother wore a beautiful sequined gown and her grandfather a lovely suit. They looked like a golden couple. They were so happy and tears of joy slid down their cheeks.

Katie's heart was overwhelmed and overflowing with joy.

The ceremony was a smash hit. They were enormously surprised and very thankful for the theme. It was as if it was Christmas 1945 again. Only this time, they had their children, grandchildren and great grandchildren there.

After the two-hour long celebration, her grandparents left to go home.

A warm smile crept on her cheeks.

She couldn't think of a more deserving couple.

Would she ever have that happiness one day?

She could only wish. But she didn't think it could ever happen for her.

***

Later, after the last holiday song played over the speaker, the barn was fairly quiet save for some chatter amongst guests who preferred to stay back and chat and glance at the colorful lights and decorations.

The family went all out for this special event. When her grandparents said they wanted to renew their vows in the barn hall where they'd first married, she knew she was going to make it special for them. They didn't want a fancy five-star luxury hotel, to them the simplicity and awesomeness of the ranch resort was all they desired.

The pastor at the church came to renew their vows. It was splendid. And speaking of which, she'd better hurry up and get back home soon so she could get some rest. She had to be up early to take her grandparents to church. It was her turn to drive them. Each of her cousins take turns. Sunday church service was everything to them.

Just then Cole came by. "You need any more help? I managed to get the rest of the equipment out."

"Oh, Cole, you've done so much, thank you."

"Hey, it's no trouble. I'm here for you...sweetie," he added with a wink.

Oh boy.

Her tummy exploded into tiny little butterflies again.

She turned around trying to hide her smile as she tended to the last table.

Just then as she folded the last tablecloth, she heard her name whispered in chatter.

"Do you really think Katie and Cole Charming are an item? I can't believe it."

Another guest whispered out loud, "Wasn't he dating that supermodel, his co-star? What was her name? Gigi?"

She turned to look at Cole. Her insides tumbled. It was true. He was a player and they all knew it. She looked like she was one of his throwaway relationships.

Had he changed?

When she looked at Cole's handsome face, she saw a muscle twitch in his jaw. He looked unimpressed.

They all knew Cole from his days in high school. It was only later that it was revealed that he was in fact, one of the many heirs to the Charming Ranch Resort, but he was still one of the boys.

"Actually, Katie's the one," he answered them in a loud confident voice. They turned around stunned, or was that embarrassed because they now knew their voices echoed in the barn hall.

"The one? You mean...you're *engaged*?" one of them had the audacity to respond.

Oh, no. Cole was going to say no.

"Yes," he said, playing along.

"Obviously this isn't the place to announce it, but yes, she's the one," he said with loving eyes and she felt it to her core.

Was he just playing?

He sure seemed convincing.

But Mistletoe was a small town and word travelled fast around there. What would her brother say to that?

He was acting, she told herself. There was nothing more to it. This was all for show and tell.

"So, we're engaged now?" she whispered to him when they were away from the group of ladies, cocking her brow. She was really beginning to enjoy this. Maybe she should get into acting too.

"And why not. If there's anything I dislike, it's nosy busy bodies," Cole said. "I have a few in my family too."

"You do?" She was surprised.

"Why does that surprise you?"

"I don't know. I figured."

"Well, there is this..." He stopped.

"There's this what?"

"Oh, nothing." He took a swig of his drink.

"You know if we're going to be married we need to stop keeping secrets." She winked.

"Yes, we do. And I'm taking you home, darling."

She fought to bite back the disappointment. He was taking her home to *her* home?

So the charade was over.

What on earth made her think there was something between them? He was only saving her face. He was into those hot skinny super models, not curvy girls like her.

"So how is this going to work exactly?" she finally asked after the last of the guests filed out and she was left alone with Cole to close up.

"Easy. I work out west. When I'm in Cali, you can just say we have a long-distance relationship. Later, you can say you ended it because of the distance. Easy fix."

Her stomach fell.

Yes, easy fix out. Katie swallowed hard. She was grateful for Cole's well-meaning spirit. So why was she hoping for more?

So much for happily ever after.

Chapter 9

"That was some party," Evan told his brother Cole, the following week. They were in the horse stall grooming the horses, getting them ready for a winter ride for the guests at the lodge. Cole loved the ranch-life and whenever he came back home to Mistletoe, he was the cowboy he always was growing up on the ranch. A part of him wondered why he left Mistletoe to chase the Hollywood lights. Nothing could compare.

"And I can't believe you're dating Mike's little sister. What did he say to that?"

"Nothing. It's fake."

"It's what?"

"No, it's not *what*, it's *fake*," Cole grinned, arching his brow.

"Yeah, funny, bro. Not. I was just about to say Mom would be thrilled. She's trying to get us all married off soon."

Cole thought for a moment.

The fake part really got to him. He wished it was for real now. But he hadn't even heard from Katie after that night.

Of course, she was busy with her wedding planning event business. He was so proud of her.

This morning, he'd asked her out for dinner and she told him she'd get back to him soon. Why did he care? Girls always threw themselves at him. But not Katie. She was different. Man, she was different. And he liked that.

Moments later, a guest came by to ride with her son. He guided them on a spectacular short trail ride.

Along the way, he helped the young boy, telling him jokes, reassuring him it's okay as it was his first horse-ride. By the end of it, the kid was laughing and having a blast. He was so gentle with the horse.

"You'd make a great father someday," the mother of the child said, after their excursion. "You're always so good with kids, Cole," the woman continued, and Cole's insides sunk.

Would he make a great father someday? He wanted to be married first. Didn't look like that would happen anytime soon.

The one woman he wanted, he couldn't have because she was off-limits, and she probably wasn't even interested in him. Besides, she deserved a man who was ready to commit to a long-term relationship. Marriage.

***

Later that afternoon, Katie parked her car near the entrance of Charming Ranch. Her heart fluttered in her chest. She was about to see that handsome cowboy who saved her from embarrassment last week.

The sound of laughter sounded from outside one barns on the grand piece of land.

She saw kids throwing snowballs at Cole and he was laughing.

"Hey, you need some help" she said.

"Just having a bit of fun," he said and dodged as they tried to pelt him with another ball.

She could see he wasn't going to fight back, not with the little kids, until...

His brother Evan came out and started hurling at him too.

Now, this time, Cole showed him a thing or two about throwing balls. Before long, all the adults were in a snowball fights with each other as the kids did the same amongst themselves.

Soon after the snowballs stopped, she saw the beautiful snowman they'd built earlier. It was magical.

"Like it?" Cole said to Katie, obviously seeing how much she admired the ginormous snowman.

There was something so familiar, so comforting about being around Cole.

"Love it. I remember when we used to make a snowman together outside the school yard and..." Their gaze locked for a moment as sprinkles of snowflakes fell around them. Was he going to kiss her? She'd heard he was an amazing kisser. Not that she ever thought about it before. Oh, who was she kidding? She'd fantasized about it ever since they were in high school. But she knew she didn't stand a chance then.

She felt as if she were in a Christmas movie and it was just the two of them.

And then...

He pulled away. He walked over to the other side of the snowman.

She looked away trying to hide the embarrassment in her face. Of course, he didn't want anything to do with her and she was after all, his best friend's younger sister.

Even though she wasn't exactly young anymore.

He only saw her as a weight-challenged geeky high school student. How could she think he would see her any differently.

"I came by to give you my answer. I'd love to have dinner with you."

"Sounds great," he said.

"And I wanted to thank you again," she said.

"For what?"

"You saved me, actually a dozen times in high school. And then again last week at the anniversary dance."

"Hey it's nothing."

Was it nothing to him?

A small part of her hoped it would be something more, such as maybe he liked her as much as she liked him.

"How about six? Should I pick you up at six?"

"Sure. I'll see you later," she replied.

Another kid came back and started throwing more snow balls, Cole looked up and laughed. "You're not gonna get me."

The kid laughed again and more came around and it started again.

Cole was in another world. And not in hers.

Chapter 10

Cole got ready for his evening with Katie.

"That's the fourth shirt you've tried on, cowboy." His brother Evan teased him. "Just don't wear a shirt then since it's bothering you."

"Nothing's bothering me," Cole lied.

"Your nose is growing, Pinocchio."

"Very funny."

"You like her, don't you?"

"She's my friend's sister. No."

"Oh, come on."

"Why do you think I like her?"

"You've mentioned her name, like oh, a hundred times this afternoon. And I saw the way you two looked at each other behind your backs."

"She looked at me?"

"Aha, you do care."

"No, I don't."

"Come on, bro. I really would like to see you happy."

Cole loved his brother, all his brothers. Especially Evan who'd been through so much. He'd lost his wife in an avalanche a while back. Ever since then, he'd been in an emotional avalanche of loneliness. He swore he'd never date again either. That was until Evan finally found someone and they'd shared that magical kiss under the mistletoe in the barn hall.

"I'm glad you're happy now, Evan. But come on, relationships are not for everyone."

"Says Mr. Romance."

"No, that's only on-screen."

And secretly in his heart. Oh, who was he kidding?

"Maybe I do like her, a little. But you know our families are close. What if it didn't work out?"

"And what if it did?"

"I don't deserve another chance. I keep screwing things up. The last thing I would want to do is break her heart."

"How?"

"I don't like to get too close to anyone. None of my relationships worked out. For too long."

"But you can change."

"Maybe I don't want to. Maybe getting close to people would mean they could hurt me."

"Or love you."

He winced.

"You know the man upstairs has a way of making a way," Evan added.

"I know," he said quietly, "Right now, bro, *I* need to make my way out on the road to pick up Katie. It's getting late."

And speaking of getting too late. Was his brother right? Could he have a second chance?

Or was it too late for him?

Chapter 11

Katie's belly knotted up in nerves.

Cole was waiting on the other side of the door.

Waves of anticipation rushed through her.

Was this a mistake? Should she date her brother's best friend? Oh, she hoped this was not a mistake. She prayed that nothing would go wrong. What could possibly go wrong? It was only a harmless little date. Not even. Just two people who know each other going out for a bite to eat. People have to eat, don't they?

Moisture clung to her palms. This was not what she wanted right now. To look and feel nervous. What was she nervous about?

She sucked in a deep breath and counted 1, 2, 3 4 then exhaled and expelled the air that was inside her.

"You know, you could always wait until tomorrow to open the door, Katie. No rush." Her roommate and friend stood at the top of the staircase looking down.

"Do you mind?" Katie said with a grin.

"I mind hearing the doorbell ring a hundred times." Her roommate said, smiling back. "Girl, I know you're nervous. No one's going to find out you two went out together to dinner. Oh, wait. It's a small town. They *will* find out.."

"What?"

"I'm teasing, girl. You're a grown woman. You should be able to do as you please."

If only.

Her roommate then left and Katie smoothed her hair again after glancing in the hallway mirror.

She finally opened the door after looking at herself in the mirror a million times.

Don't look too eager. Don't look too eager.

The tall, dark and handsome cowboy stood before her and her pulse pounded hard and fast in her veins. He had a lovely bouquet of flowers in his hands.

Oh, my.

He looked stunning and captivating in his jacket and crisp pants, his buckle so shiny, and his cowboy boots looked pristine. He tilted his cowboy hat to greet her. A cute grin perched on his lovely lips. Would she ever know what they really feel like. Right now, she knew how she felt.

He tilted his cowboy hat. "Good evening, Ms Smythe."

"Cole! You look amazing! Please come in."

Too eager. Too eager.

"So do you. You look beautiful. And these are for you," he said, in his deep lovely voice as he walked into the foyer. He handed her the lovely flowers. She inhaled the sweet fragrance. His sweet smile crinkled the corners of his eyes. For a moment, their eyes locked.

"Thank you. They're gorgeous."

A magical pulse was felt between them, at least that's what she believed.

"You really look amazing, Katie," he said again, his voice deeper.

They were inches apart. Was he going to kiss her? She sure hoped so, but then again it would be too soon. Well, twenty years in the waiting was not exactly too soon. Still, the memories of Cole rescuing her out of terrible situations when she was a geeky kid back in high school, long before geeky was a thing to be admired in this tech age we're living in. He was always there for her, respecting her, encouraging her and just being his wonderful self—and he was also sought after by all the popular girls in school. To which she was none of that.

And now, he was there, in her rental home she shared with two other roommates so she could afford the rent while her business took off.

"Are you ready?"

"Yes, I'll put these in a vase first." She hurried off to the kitchen to place the flowers in a vase after taking them out of their wrapper.

"I'm ready. Let's go," she said, moments later. And she didn't know if she'd ever be ready.

Chapter 12

"Hmm, the food is delicious," Katie said, after she'd finished taking a few bites into her juicy steak and creamy-rich mashed potatoes.

Cole took her to the Mistletoe Steak House. The best in town.

She told him she remembered going there as a child. She also thanked him again.

"For saving me, like always." Her smile was pretty, as her lips, as her personality. There wasn't anything he didn't like about her.

"You saved *me*," he told her. "Helped me too when I wanted to fight...got me thinking about my future. That's one of the reasons I took drama. Drama therapy dealing with being adopted and wondering what happened to my biological folks. It gave me a chance to be in control of the narrative. To be someone else. Sure beats fighting. Got a lot of frustration and anger out...at what happened in the past. But we can't live in the past. You taught me that. To look to the future."

"And you found Hollywood."

"I guess you could say that. Or Hollywood found me."

What was with him?

He never spilled his guts to anyone, especially not a lady. But he felt so comfortable around Katie. He always did. And he didn't want anything to ruin their friendship. Nothing at all.

The following day, they had a day filled with surprises as the snow fell over Mistletoe creating a blanket of white and a bright experience. They laughed and built another snowman on the ranch, then they went back to feed the horses in the stalls. She helped Cole fix the decorations around the stall.

That afternoon, they brought gifts to the Children's Hospital surgery wing.

Later that evening, they walked through the Mistletoe Antique Market, one of the largest in the region.

"Such a lovely couple," a store clerk said to them after Cole left her a huge tip. He always liked to give back.

Later, it was chilly. She forgot her gloves.

"You're hands look cold."

"I'm okay."

"Come on," he sang. "Put your hands in my arms."

His grin was so cute and dimpled his cheeks.

"Okay."

She placed her hands in the crux of his arms and they were nice and warm. His strength made her feel warm, comforted.

***

Later, they saw Mike and his wife, shopping too.

Oh, this is not good.

Mike's sister was cozying up with Cole in the market. Now, Mike was going to know something was up between Cole and Katie.

Just then Mike stood before them, the look of shock in his eyes. "Katie? Cole?"

"Mike," Katie began, pulling her hands out of Cole's jacket.

"Hey man, it's not what it looks like."

An awkward pause grabbed the moment then...

"Isn't it?" Mike said, his eyes looking wild now.

"Your sister was shopping and I offered to help her." He didn't want to mention the part about him taking her to dinner too, not just yet.

Mike's wife looked concerned. "Everything all right between you two?"

"I don't think so, because it looks like someone doesn't understand the meaning of honor. Dating a friend's little sister is never cool."

"What's not cool is how you're handling this."

"Mike, I can make my own decisions," Katie said. "Please don't embarrass me out here."

"I'm not, sis. But you shouldn't be..." Mike fumbled for words, his face reddening like Santa's suit.

"I'm leaving town soon," Cole finally said. The last thing on earth he wanted was to mess up his friendship with Mike and more importantly make things awkward for Katie. He was no good for her. It's just no use.

"It's... just a friendly visit." Cole was serious. He didn't want to ruin their relationship. "My agent called me this morning. I'm heading back west now."

"So soon?" Mike asked.

He saw the look of hurt on Katie's face. The last thing he wanted to do was to hurt Katie. But it was too late. He'd already done that.

Chapter 13

Katie's heart tumbled in her chest.

He was leaving her? Of course he was. It was just a friendly date, nothing more.

"So you're spending Christmas in Cali?" Mike asked.

"Yep. Looks like they're beginning production again."

"I thought Hollywood closed down during the holidays."

"Yes, but I've been asked to come back to reshoot some scenes," he said. It wasn't completely a lie, though usually, there was no filming taking place in his production.

"Oh, okay," Mike said, reluctantly. "Well, see you around then."

"Sure thing."

Well, that was awkward. But once again, disaster averted.

***

Later in the week, at the Christmas Eve Barn Hall Dance, Katie looked at the happy faces. She'd already told the Charmings she'd be there.

But the truth was, she was feeling lost since Cole took a flight back to California. Could this Christmas get any worse? She thought it would be the best Christmas ever. But she was mistaken.

The wedding planner who would never have her own wedding. Was that her destiny?

"Sorry, you're feeling down," Mike said.

"Mike, I'm surprised you're here."

"Look, sis. Everything's gonna be okay."

239

"Really, Mike. I appreciate that you're always looking out for me. I really do, but you've got to let me live my own life. You can't go chasing away guys that might be..."

"Might be...?"

"I like Cole. I've liked him for as long as I can remember. I know you feel he wouldn't be the right guy for me, but I think you went and chased him away. He doesn't want to ruin your friendship or the business you've got going."

"He told you about that, huh?"

"Yes, I think it's great what you're doing to help young people in the community."

"Thanks. You know how I feel about my friends dating my sisters."

"I know. But have you asked how *we* feel about it?"

"You're right."

He placed his drink down.

"I have a Christmas present for you," he said. "You and I are exchanging gifts. I hope you like it."

"I'm sure I will."

Later, after all the guests were called to the Christmas Wish Tree to exchange gifts. She picked out her box and gave it to Mike."

"Thanks, sis."

"Where's my present?"

"Here." He handed her a small box.

It was very tiny. She smiled and said thank you. When she opened the box, it was empty. Then she saw a note attached to the top of the box. She opened it and her jaw fell open.

Chapter 14

Katie rushed outside the barn and didn't have to go far.

A smile as wide as the Mistletoe River crossed her lips.

"Cole!"

"Katie!"

They both embraced and hugged each other so tight, she could feel his energy.

Just then Mike came out of the barn. "Hope you like it."

"I don't get it," Katie said.

"I told your brother how I really feel about you and how much I would never hurt you," Cole said. "I also told him I thought..." He then turned to her. "You're the most beautiful woman in the world, Katie. I would like to spend more time with you."

"But what about Hollywood?"

"Hollywood can wait. It's only once in a lifetime you get the chance to spend time with the most amazing woman in the world. I'd made some mistakes in the past and wished I could turn back the time. But I realized that I don't have to. I could make that change now. My wish was always to be with that special person. And it looked as if the man upstairs heard my wish and made it come true. I would love to be with you and get to know you more, if you...Would you like that?"

"I would love nothing more."

Later, after dancing, Cole and Katie ended up under that famous mistletoe in the barn hall.

"Well, look at that," she said.

"I know," he said, in a low voice. "I feel like the luckiest cowboy in the world. I have the most beautiful woman in the world—inside and out."

He leaned down and gave her a soft, beautiful kiss that felt like magic. She treasured it and wanted it to last even longer. His lips were soft and tender. Waves of delight slid down her back.

"Katie, I'd love to spend more time with you," he said.

"Oh, Cole." She felt warm and joyful inside. "I'd love to spend more time with you, too."

She hugged him realizing she *did* have the best Christmas ever. A new beginning. And a new love.

***

***

Thank you for reading *Rescued by the Cowboy at Christmas Books 1-4)*. To be notified of future stories, you can send us an email at pageturningstories@gmail.com .

Books by J. A. Somers

Rescued by the Cowboy at Christmas
Cowboy Under the Mistletoe
Cowboy's Christmas Blessing
Cowboy for Christmas
Cowboy's Christmas Wish

Milton Keynes UK
Ingram Content Group UK Ltd.
UKHW011940240823
427419UK00001B/15